CREATIVE LOVE

J. NICHOLE

not the lost page

Copyright © 2018 by J. Nichole

All rights reserved.

No part of this book may be reproduced in any form or by any electronic or mechanical means, including information storage and retrieval systems, without written permission from the author, except for the use of brief quotations in a book review.

❦ Created with Vellum

For my angel baby, may I always make you proud.

J. NICHOLE NEWSLETTER

I'd love to keep in contact with you, and if you feel the same, join my newsletter.

www.NotTheLastPage.com/by-jnichole

Chapter One
BRYAN

"Will he be here through the weekend?" With one eye open I pull my head off the couch and study Laila. She's standing beside my brother looking up at him while she shuffles papers across the kitchen counter.

Chris shrugs his shoulders and replies, "I was hoping he'd be gone already." When I clear my throat they both look toward me. The irritation etched over my brother's face is undeniable. "Oh did we wake you?" He no longer looks like my kid brother who indulged himself with candy and junk food when he was growing up.

Sitting up with my back against the couch I grab my shirt that I threw in a heap on the floor after the club last night. "You could use more practice on your inside voice."

Chris' biceps bulge and his eyebrow twitches. It's been years since we've been under the same roof for more than just a few days. It doesn't help that their apartment is hardly large enough for the two of them. "Didn't know I had to whisper in my own house." Laila slaps Chris' arm.

"You two argue like school kids." She sits beside me on the couch curling her short legs under her getting cozy.

"Just found out yesterday that I have to work this weekend." She looks between Chris and me.

"Too bad. I was hoping you could give me the female perspective on the apartments I plan to look at this weekend." A small smile spreads across her face. "That excited to get me out of here?"

She laughs and throws up her hand. "No, I was going to ask you if you would mind entertaining Nicole this weekend while I'm at work." She looks away from me. "I'm sure she wouldn't mind giving you a female perspective."

Clapping my hands together I shout, "Hell no I wouldn't mind."

"Wait do you remember Nicole?" I visited Chris on campus a few times, and while there, I met Laila. The women at Lee University were all sexy. I don't know how my brother managed to stay faithful to Laila. I should have gone to a black college; maybe I would have graduated. Instead I went to University of Tennessee and dropped out after my second year.

"No, but if she kicks it with you I'm sure she's cool. And if she went to Lee I'm sure she's sexy." I grin rubbing my hands together. "Big, small, petite, tall I like them all." Laila bursts out laughing. My brother groans from the kitchen.

"That's your problem," Chris mumbles.

Ignoring his comment Laila says, "She'll be here tomorrow. I'll tell her to catch a Moovn to the apartment." She peers beyond me to look at Chris. "Bae will you be home to introduce Bryan to Nicole?" Chris nods his head. "You've been here long enough to know where you can take her. Maybe take her out to dinner, get some drinks. Whatever." I nod my head and Laila stands up from the couch walking the short distance to their room. "Oh and thanks," she offers before disappearing.

Chris hovers over me. "Listen, Nicole is the girl who

helped orchestrate me getting back with Laila. She's cool so don't fuck her over." His stern look reminds me of our mother.

"Damn dude. Chill out. I wouldn't do that to Laila's girl." His eyebrows arch. "Do you have that list of places for me to look at?"

"Yeah I'll leave it out on the counter." He walks to the window and stares out. "You sure you want to move here?"

I left Tennessee after abruptly quitting my job at our family's business. I never had it in me to be a businessman in an office. Although I wanted to do what I could to help the firm grow even more, I never planned to make it my lifetime career, unlike Chris, who my dad expects to take over once he retires. "What better place than New York for an artist?"

"You think you'll be able to afford living in New York from the art projects you commission?"

I shrug my shoulders and say, "I can live like a starving artist if it means I'll be able to do what I want to do and not what Dad expects me to do."

"What happened that day you quit?" I haven't shared the story with Chris. The day I showed up at his doorstep with a suitcase, I just said I needed a place to crash. With little hesitation, he's let me stay on the couch for the last two weeks.

"That's a story that needs a bottle of Hennessy." Looking at the time on my phone I say, "And you should probably get to work. I'm sure Dad will be upset if you miss the morning check-in." I grin knowing my brother, although continuing the family business, even expanding it here to New York, would much rather be doing anything else.

He shakes his head. "Maybe one day I'll have the gusto to be like you." We both chuckle at the irony. Chris and I share genes, but our looks and personality vary on separate ends of the spectrum. We personify the meaning of night and day.

Alone in the living room, I examine the empty walls. After a year of being in this apartment they are still bare. Opening my photo app, I scroll through my artwork. Any of the pieces would liven this place up. In my haste, I left the artwork at my studio in Tennessee. Eventually I'll need to return to gather the rest of my shit. I definitely need to collect my artwork, if nothing else. I have art pieces to sell to garner cash for the next few months at least.

A text message comes through from an unknown number.

222-365-1809: can I see you today?

I'm sure it's someone I met in my escapades here in New York. I try to make the chicks I meet feel special by giving them my number after beating their back out. I don't ever save theirs though. Keeps me from calling for a repeat experience. They rarely ever contact me. Chicks have something against calling guys if they don't call first. It's worked for me.

Chris: must not have saved your number, who is this?
222-365-1809: Jenna, met at the bar last weekend...

Yeah, Jenna, she was bad too. She has thick hips and breasts that bounced around like balloons while she rode me.

Chris: where do you want to meet?

I bought her a whiskey sour at the bar where she was celebrating with her homegirls. She was appreciative but ignored me in favor of her girls. When they started to leave, she slipped in the seat to my right and chatted me up. She is sexy and witty, a bad ass combination. If I ever wanted to chill out with one girl she'd be a good candidate. But I don't, and if we fuck again I'll make sure she knows.

222-365-1809: my place?
Chris: be there in an hour?

222-365-1809: see you soon

Laila and Chris have been holed up in the room but Chris should be leaving soon. After sniffing my armpit, I hop off the couch and knock on their door. I hear them moving around and hope I'm not disrupting their morning sex. Neither responds and I knock again. I smell like the subway. Coming in late from the club left me without an option to wake Chris and Laila for a shower. I have to find my own place tomorrow. I raise my fist again but Chris opens the door. With his head cocked he says, "You need the bathroom?"

I nod my head as Laila walks between us. "See you when I get off." Kissing Chris on the lips, she then pats my arm before she leaves.

I smile at Chris still standing in the doorway. "Were y'all fucking?" He rolls his eyes and shakes his head. "See that's why I won't settle down. I like spontaneous sex."

Chris moves aside and says over his shoulder, "You'll find any excuse to stay single. The right girl will come along and turn your world upside down." He pauses. "Again." I ignore his comment, surely in reference to Shelby. Her name alone, invading my thoughts, makes me cringe after all these years.

I let the thoughts of her drift away in the lukewarm shower, another reason my apartment hunt has to be successful. I miss hot showers. Climbing out of the shower, I make an executive decision to boycott the subway. Public transportation will be the one thing I hate about city living. My Audi A5 is sitting in my driveway back in Tennessee but will probably have to stay right there. I download the Moovn app Laila mentioned to schedule a pick up. I also send a text to Jenna asking for her address.

My Moovn driver arrives and gets me to her place a few minutes shy of the hour I promised. When she opens the door my eyes scan her body. She isn't hiding the reason she summoned me to her apartment. With a silk robe over her body, her perky nipples reveal she's bare beneath the robe. I reach out and brush my hand across her chin. "Can I come in?" She nods her head and opens the door for me to walk through.

I walk, from memory, to her bed. Standing at the footboard, I turn around and admire the rest of the studio. In the light, I'm able to see the galley kitchen against the wall, and a small couch sits alone near the window. Jenna steps in front of me and de-robes, taking my attention away from her bare apartment. Again my eyes scan her body, this time in its naked form.

For a woman who sits at a desk most of the day, her body is in phenomenal shape. A cross encircled by roses flanks her stomach. She takes a deep breath as I trace her tattoo with the tip of my finger. Leaning into her, I encircle her lips, biting her bottom lip and licking the inside of her mouth. I grab a handful of her coils, pulling her closer to me, and her hard nipples insult my chest.

I pull apart and whisper, "Is this why you wanted me to come over," into her ear. She steps away from me and stares into my eyes. She nods. Intertwining her fingers with mine, I look down at the connection. Our fingers overlapping, both golden brown, only her manicured nails set our hands apart. She guides me to the bed, laying down in front of me. She reaches for my pants, unbuckling them as I step out of my boots. My pants drop below my waist as I pull my shirt over my head.

Jenna reaches up and wraps her hands around my forearms, pulling softly but aggressively. I lay on top of her and reach my fingers between her legs. She's ready. But instead of indulging, I kiss her neck, then her nipples. Licking my tongue into her belly button I continue my expedition down her stomach, stopping at the crutch of her pussy. I look up at her and beyond the humps of her chest I see her squirm, her head moving side to side as I breathe onto her clit.

I open her folds and lick between them as I listen to Jenna moan. Her moans grow louder with each flick of my tongue. When her legs begin to dance, flapping side to side, I climb her body. Beside her pillow I grab the condom she placed knowingly. Rolling it on before she loses her climax, I thrust inside of her. Her hips rise to meet mine.

Unlike our first night where I fucked her hard and quick, I'm taking my time. Her hands roam my chest. She pushes me off her and in one swift move she mounts me. I let her take control but use my hands to guide her hips to bring the amount of friction I need to cum.

With my eyes half open and my jaw tense, I watch her closely, waiting for her to ride herself to ecstasy. Eyes closed and mouth parted her head flings back and that's when I know it's coming. I hold her hips and push into her once, then again. Her body quivers as I clinch my mouth and my dick pulsates inside of her. She collapses onto my chest, her breathing erratic. I wrap my arms around her, holding her tight. With my nose buried into her coils, the colorful art on the wall beside me catches my eye. I need to tell her this is the last time. Instead of verbalizing the obvious, I clear my throat and say, "I need to get out of here."

She rolls onto the mattress, reaching for the sheet to cover her body. With her hand raised, she waves her fingers. Jenna stretches out with the manufactured art as her backdrop. While pulling my shirt over my head I ask, "Can I replace that piece?"

She looks behind her and says, "That one?" While pointing to the piece on the wall, I nod my head.

Chapter Two
NICOLE

"No offense to you," I take Bryan in from his sly smile to his broad shoulders and skin that reminds me of cinnamon, "but I can't believe Laila is leaving me to her boyfriend's brother." Chris apologizes again. I cut my eyes at him. "Tickets from Atlanta aren't cheap. Who knows the next time I'll be in New York to visit her ass." I finally finished my degree from Lee in the spring. I didn't necessarily want to return to Atlanta but couldn't pass up the opportunity to work for the Taylor Corporation. After my roommates watched me cross the stage, the last of the four of us to graduate, we promised we'd make our rounds to visit each other. Laila in New York, Jennifer in Texas, and Monica in California for her medical program. Getting around to each of them won't be cheap.

"You're here now. Might as well make the best of it." Bryan walks toward me with his hand outstretched. I take his hand in mine and the warmth from his palm calms my level of pissivity.

I take a deep breath and say, "What the hell. Might as well." I arch my brow. "You've been here for a few weeks."

"A few weeks too long," Chris shouts from the bedroom.

Bryan shrugs his shoulders. "He's just mad cause I'm cock blocking." He grabs my suitcase from the front door and places it near the coffee table. The couch would have been fine for me for the weekend but now that plan makes me feel claustrophobic.

Bryan tries to find a corner for my bag. "Chris, what's going on with these bare walls?" I ask from the kitchen.

Bryan pushes my bag under the window seal. "I was thinking the same thing." He points to the wall. "When I bring my art from my studio I'll hook them up."

Laila hasn't shared much information about Bryan with me, other than that he's the free spirit out of the Clark brothers. She was amused, but not surprised, when he showed up on their doorstep after quitting the firm. "Art studio?" I watch his face light up with the widest smile he's had since I've been here.

"I'll tell you more while we eat." He looks at his watch. "I'm sure you are hungry by now, right?"

"I could eat." I smile while he grabs his wallet from the table.

"Laila should be here when y'all get back." Chris stands in the doorway of the bedroom as Bryan and I walk to the front door.

"If not I'll need you to give me the address of that office." I frown. "I'll have to drag her out of there."

Chris laughs and Bryan closes the door behind us. On our way to the elevator Bryan fumbles with his phone. "You good?" He looks up from the phone and his straight face confirms his focus.

"There's this restaurant I want to try out but it's in Manhattan. I scheduled a car pickup." New York is infamous for the subway. Laila's explained how she's learned how to navigate her way from Brooklyn to Manhattan for work. Her descriptions of eccentric riders and piss-filled air doesn't sound ideal but she seems to manage.

"Why not the subway?"

The elevator doors open and we step inside. "Scrubbing my skin off to remove the stench of the train after each ride? I decided it's not for me."

I watch as his face sours. He and Chris resemble each other but not enough for me to believe they were brothers if I saw them on the street. "I think I need the full New York experience. Subway included."

"The car should be outside by the time we exit the building." He cocks his head toward me. "But if you insist on the experience, who am I to deny you?" I'm oddly excited, smiling as we exit the elevator. "But not till after dinner. I'll need a few drinks to make it bearable."

On our ride to Manhattan, Bryan acts as tour guide making up historical facts, and pointing out bars he's been to each night. "Meeting a girl in each?" I stare out the window as we cross the Brooklyn Bridge.

"I've met a few." The traffic comes to a stop. "What about you? Do you have a guy in Atlanta?"

I shake my head, maybe too emphatically, causing Bryan to laugh. I haven't dated anyone for more than a few weeks consecutively in a couple of years. Relationships don't work for me. I invest too much, too soon, and the guys aren't ever ready to commit. Fucking and leaving them seems to work better for me. Get in and get out before my heart gets involved, before I have the chance to get hurt. "Single and always mingling."

Bryan grins. "We'll see if we can find someone for you to mingle with tonight." I expected Bryan to shoot his shot, but it is better to know now he isn't interested. I look his way and imagine his goatee rubbing between my legs. Too bad.

The driver stops along a road in an area that looks residential. Bryan and I exchange a look before he leans over the seat to ask, "Are you sure this is the place?" The driver nods his head and unlocks the door. Bryan holds the door open for me then laughs. "Did we just get booted out of his car?"

"He wasn't interested in answering any questions." I shrug. "Guess he did his job. If we were on the subway, we could have found a nice patron to guide us in the right direction."

Bryan shakes his head. "For a small fee I'm sure any of the bums would be willing to guide us to our final destination."

We look up and down the street before Bryan recognizes the small signage for the restaurant he chose. Inside the restaurant is nothing I expected. There are two top tables and an expansive bar stretching across the side. The oregano and basil scents prevail and I look around at the plates in front of people while the hostess directs us to our table.

Bryan orders a bottle of wine and looks to me, "Are you okay with white wine?"

"Sure." I examine the menu and find an eggplant parmesan dish. Bryan orders an appetizer for us to share. Once the waitress walks away I ask him how he'll make a living now that he quit his job.

"I'm going to open an art studio. Commission art work." His fingers twirl around the candle sitting in the middle of the table. "I've always wanted to do my art full time. No time like the present."

"Is that why you quit?" A group of guys laugh at the bar. I try to see them through the dim light with no luck.

Bryan follows my gaze and says, "There you go." He nods toward the guys. "One of them can be the guy you mingle with this weekend."

I look at the candle between us and say, "Except it looks like we are on a date."

He twists his lips around. "I could say you are my little sister." He leans back in his seat. "Sis, did Mom send any of her scrub with you?" His voice carries over the soft Italian music playing. I look from him to the couple sitting beside us. They stare at me as they wait for my response. "Her scrub is the only thing that keeps my skin smooth."

"Yeah she sent a couple of jars but said next time you have to pay. She said she can't keep playing bingo if you don't pay her." He coughs and covers his mouth. "You know she loves bingo. In fact, you owe me a couple of dollars cause I had to front your scrub habit."

"Remind me before I drop you off at the airport." The waitress places our appetizer between us and lets Bryan taste the wine.

"They aren't even looking this way. What now?" He leans back in his chair and stares at the bar. He grabs a stuffed mushroom and pops it into his mouth.

"This is what you have to do." He grabs my glass from the table and hands it to me. "Walk over there with your glass and..." he shakes his head. "No, no glass." He takes the glass back from me setting it down. "Walk over to the bar and ask for a bottle of Perrier."

"Ask for a bottle of water from the bartender?" I look toward the bar again. "Are you sure you pick up women at the bar?" His mouth drops. "I hope you're better on your own cause you're a horrible wing man."

"Just try it." He taps the table. "If it doesn't work I'll buy your meals all weekend."

I stand up and straighten my sweater. "Deal." I don't turn down a challenge. Besides I could use a sugar daddy for the weekend. I walk over to the bar, keeping my eye on the group of guys. I find a spot beside the group and lean over the bar, putting my tits on display. After the bartender leaves to grab my bottle of water, one of them asks if I'm from the area. Before I can turn and walk away with my bottle of water he has my phone number.

Gritting my teeth I return to the table. As I take my seat I feel Bryan staring at me. When I realize the guys from the bar are no longer looking in my direction I look to Bryan and whisper, "Not my type."

His eyebrows raise. "What is your type?"

Leaning across the table with my tits resting near my plate I say, "Athletic." My eyes gaze across his biceps. "Taller than me, professional, funny, confident but not cocky." Our eyes connect and I continue, "Decent dude."

He adjusts in his seat. "And if that guy came around you'd just want to fuck?" The lady sitting across from us looks at Bryan with her mouth slightly open. I return her stare until she turns back to her food. "I mean, seems like any of those guys could work you over for the weekend, right?"

"I don't know about you, but I'm not out here just fucking every dude who wants to fuck." I keep my voice low to not disturb the people around us. "I just don't want to be in a relationship."

The waitress places our entrees on the table and we take a few bites before Bryan's curiosity gets the best of him. "And if a guy comes around and doesn't just want to fuck?"

"Can't speak in hypotheticals, Bryan." I take a small bite of my eggplant parmesan, letting my mouth linger over the fork. "If it ever happened, maybe I would consider a relationship."

Chapter Three
BRYAN

So don't fuck her over. Chris' warning haunts me as I watch Nicole's lips while she sips on the glass of wine. I'd much rather take her back to the apartment and let those same lips wrap around my...

Nicole taps on the table to get my attention. "Are you ready for the check, sir?" The waitress is staring at me waiting for a reply.

"Sorry. Guess I was in another place." I look at Nicole again and she shrugs her shoulders. "Yes, let's get the check."

When the waitress walks away Nicole calls my bluff. "In another place, huh?" She purses her lips and I lick my lips in return. "Looks like you were dreaming of someone special with that grin on your face. Someone has become more than just a fuck buddy." My eyes grow wide. "Look at you. Nervous and everything."

"Is that what you think?" I shake my head. "Not at all."

Nicole looks down at her phone. "What's next?" We stand up after paying the bill and I lead her to the door.

She takes one last look at the bar before exiting. Maybe

she was more interested in that guy than she led me to believe. I watch her hips sway as she walks in front of me, giving me more of a view than when she walked to the bar. Each step she takes makes me want to ignore my little brother's threat more.

"Dinner was savory. But I hope you have room left in that belly for something sweet." Nicole's eyes perk up and she nods her head. "Good, I've also wanted to try Junior's Cheesecake." Nicole looks at me with a blank expression and I'm reminded of our age difference. "You know the place from Making the Band?" Still nothing. "Diddy's show?"

Nicole laughs and grabs her side. "I was waiting to see if you were going to school me on Diddy." She holds her head up high. "I'm young but not that young. I know what you are talking about."

I poke her in the side. "Had me feeling extra old." The sun is beginning to set and the chill in the air is perfect for a walk. "Feel like walking?" Before she responds I look down at her shoes.

She lifts a foot off the ground and waves her classic Adidas in front of me. "Brought my walking shoes. I'm super prepared for this New York experience."

The residential vibe is replaced with lights and loud noise. We pass street performers and Nicole stops and looks on, grabbing my arm as one guy does a flip over another's back. "They are amazing."

The street performers continue as the crowd grows around us, forcing us to stand closer. Instead of watching the acrobatics with amazement, I'm intrigued by Nicole's reactions. With each flip, dance move, or beat by the drummer her body moves. Her back arches or her hips sway. She moves away from me then right back in place, never once releasing my arm.

The crowd erupts in applause and Nicole joins them.

She reaches in her purse, dropping a couple of dollars into the bucket for the performers. We continue walking to Junior's and we both point out different sites. I point out things I know she wouldn't see in Atlanta and watch as her face lights up each time.

"We can ride on one of those before you leave and get an official tour of the city," I say as I point to a double decker tour bus.

"Before I leave?" Nicole stops walking. "Laila better not be working the entire time I'm here. I'd hate to monopolize your entire weekend." She looks down at her Adidas.

"Really?" She looks up at me and the kid-like amazement has disappeared. "I don't have a job. Don't have anywhere else to be this weekend." I start walking and she follows behind me. "Entertaining you is cool." I hear her snicker. "Besides we have to get you sexed up before you leave." She slaps my back, causing me to lunge forward, leaving her laughing behind me.

"Wait." She yells. "There it is." I turn around and look at her waiting for her to explain further. "Junior's." I look in the direction she's staring and see the line forming outside of the restaurant.

"Guess we weren't the only ones in search of good cheesecake." We approach the line with apprehension. "We could get something else if you don't feel like waiting."

She grabs her phone and then looks back to the line. "Laila hasn't texted yet. I asked her to let me know when she's leaving her office and I would meet her back at the apartment."

"Junior's it is then." I turn to look at her. "Tell me about your time at L. U. "

She squints her eyes before asking, "What do you want to know?"

"From the looks of this line we may be here for a while. Tell me anything."

"The four plus years I spent at L. U. were some of the best years of my life. Of course meeting the girls was the highlight." She takes a breath. "Wish I would have concentrated more on selecting a major. Would have graduated on time."

"At least you finished." From the wince I could tell she didn't care for that response. "Let me guess. Everyone tells you that?"

"Something like that. Everyone except for my parents. My dad wasn't happy about footing the bill for another year of school."

"Parents have a strange way of making their kids feel inadequate." I whisper. "How'd you meet Laila and the rest of them?"

"Wait. What was that you whispered about parents?" Her eyebrows gather and she looks to me for a response.

I exhale and contemplate giving her a surface answer. I'd rather not discuss my issues with my dad here, definitely not now. "Nothing. I just know how parents can be."

"Hmm. I'll let that go for now." We step a few feet toward the entrance of Junior's. "Jennifer was my roommate, and she met Laila during freshman orientation. Naturally I met Laila through Jennifer." I nod my head as the pieces begin to connect. "Monica was Laila's roommate."

"Did y'all ever have any cat fights?" I can't imagine Laila or Nicole having an issue with anyone. They seem to be the type to be non-confrontational and get along with everyone. But then again, Laila did slap the shit out of Chris' ex from what I have heard.

"Not between the four of us." She rolls her eyes up. "Not anything significant enough to remember." She laughs. "But I'm sure you've heard about Laila's run-ins with Chris' ex-girlfriend." I nod my head. "Laila can be feisty if she needs to be."

"Certainly would fool me. Had my brother not given me the details of her slapping Courtney I would never think she could be angered."

"We all have our breaking point, right?"

"Absolutely." I examine her, looking at her facial expression that is soft and measured. She's standing with her arms loosely crossed across her chest. "What do you think your breaking point would be?"

"I'm hoping to avoid most of my breaking points by staying single. Other than that, I think being overlooked at work would be my breaking point."

"What type of work do you do?" She frowns. "That exciting, huh?"

"It's not what I imagined I'd be doing when I graduated. I can't complain because I get paid. But it's not exciting one bit." She makes eye contact and continues, "Tell me about you. Where'd you go to school?"

"I went to University of Tennessee. But I didn't graduate." Nicole's face doesn't return the response I was expecting. She waits for me to give her more details. "Dropped out after my sophomore year."

"Ever consider finishing?" We are at the front of the line and the hostess interrupts us asking if we'll be dining in or picking up. Nicole looks around the restaurant and says, "Dining in."

When we are seated at the table I say, "If this art thing sustains me." I shake my head. "I don't plan on it."

We study the bakery menu before the server returns. I ask her, "Which one are you going to try?"

She sighs. "I hate when a menu has too many options." I nod in agreement. "I think I'll go with the strawberry." She looks at me with a grin. "Can't go wrong with the classic."

I point at myself. "I was going to go with the strawberry but I don't want to have the same as you." I search the menu again for a different option.

"We can both have strawberry. If it is good I would hate for you to think I'll give mine up."

I laugh at her honesty. "Fair enough." The waitress returns to the table and we order two strawberry cheesecakes.

"Tell me more." Nicole looks at me over a huge chunk of cheesecake with a strawberry perched on top. The things I could do with that strawberry and those lips.

"I was working with the family business until recently." I stretch my arms out wide. "Now I'm here." Her eyebrow raises. "What?"

"That's like me saying I was born and now I'm here." She wags her finger at me. "There's much more sandwiched in there." She looks around us. "We have time."

"When I was in high school, I was a jock. Played football all four years." She examines me. I don't have my young athletic body anymore but I spend a fair amount of time in the gym. My shoulders are still broad and my six pack isn't defined but visible. "In college is when I gave up the sports and picked up the brush."

Her head tilts backwards. "You weren't creative before college?"

"I could draw. I would draw Anime characters all the time."

"Ani who?" She looks at me with skepticism.

"Are you trying to play me again?" I laugh and she shakes her head. "*Dragonball Z* ring a bell?"

"Not a single one. But maybe it was a guy thing. In high school I was watching *Gilmore Girls* and *The O. C.*" She cocks her head at me. "Do you know either of those shows?"

"Nope. We'll leave it at our gender being the main differentiator. I refuse to believe I'm getting old."

Nicole stops taking bites midway through her cheesecake and sits back. She watches the people around us. The people who were once beside us have since left and a new wave of patrons have filled the tables.

"Okay, tour guide. I think you owe me a trip on the subway." She puts her hand in the air and says, "But first we have to get you liquored up, right?"

I nod my head with enthusiasm. "That's the only way I'm volunteering to torture myself." Instead of finding a bar in Times Square where it will be filled with tourists, I request a Moovn ride.

On our ride back to Brooklyn, the views we saw before are illuminated with lights and New York looks alive. As we approach the Brooklyn Bridge, Nicole turns around and catches a picture of the city behind us. She leans into me with her camera outstretched and before I can recoil she snaps a picture of the two of us. Grabbing the camera from her I say, "Give me your best pose."

She leans against the door and with her head tilted away she looks back at me. I snap the picture before she begins to laugh. "Something about the city gives me energy."

The driver pulls up to the bar that I requested in the app, and instead of not knowing where we are, I exit the car with confidence. I've been here before.

I lead us directly to the bar where the guys sitting around aren't as lively as the guys at the Italian restaurant. Nicole sits beside me and all eyes are on us until we order our first drink. I'm surprised when she orders a Hennessy with a splash of Coke.

She raises her glass to me and says, "To New York."

I tap her glass and respond, "To New York." My eyes grow wide when she effortlessly takes a sip. "This is going to be a fun night," I whisper.

Chapter Four
NICOLE

"I should probably stop at two." I wave my hand in front of Bryan to reject the next drink he's passing my way. I outstretch my hand to the mock dance floor and say, "Can you dance?"

He puts the glass in front of him and shrugs his shoulders. "I can do a little something."

I nod toward the dance floor as the beat of the next song drops. I'm not familiar with the song but I can two-step to just about anything. The crowd in the bar has grown but the vibe is still laid back, with the exception of the group of females getting their life on the dance floor. I'm surprised when Bryan grabs me by the waist and turns me around.

My hips lean into him but I keep some space between us. He whispers in my ear, "Show these girls what you got." I laugh as I look over my shoulder.

We maintain our rhythm, keeping up with the group of girls. Then either my two drinks kick in or the Beyoncé song motivates me, but I thrust my hips into Bryan and dance like my life depends on it, grinding and gyrating into his groin with his hands sitting slightly on my hips.

By the end of the song, I'm hot and somewhat bothered and I take Bryan's hand to lead him back to the bar. I grab the bartender's attention and ask for a glass of water. When I turn around I see a woman leaning into Bryan's ear. I try to avoid staring at them, but can't turn away.

The woman is wearing a skin tight dress with cutouts around her waist and when she places her arm up to Bryan's shoulder I see an intricate cross tattoo through one of the cutouts. Her hair, a curly fro, blocks my view of her face. Bryan looks back to me and I divert my eyes and focus on the glass of water in my hands.

"Nicole." I look up to see Bryan standing closer. Between myself and the curly fro. When he steps to the side she's smiling with her hand outstretched.

I take her hand as Bryan says, "This is Jenna." Jenna. That's it. Without an accompanying title. "I was just telling her about the day we've had." The smile on his face grows.

"Oh. It's been awesome." I look to her with confusion. Not sure if I should be refraining from cock blocking or marking my territory. "Bryan is a great tour guide."

"I bet he is," Jenna says observing me the way I observed her. "Don't forget the painting you want to replace in my apartment. I've been staring at it with skepticism since you pointed it out."

"Art has its way of changing forms." Bryan stands beside me and says, "I'll let you know when I have my pieces here and you can pick something."

She nods and waves, walking away from us. My eyes follow her until she disappears into the darkness of the bar. I turn to Bryan and ask, "One of your flings?" He nods his head. "Did you tell her I was your sister?"

He looks at me with his eyes drawn together. "Why would I do that?"

I shrug my shoulders. "So she doesn't think you're on a date."

"No. That was only for you to get some dick. Crazy phenomenon between men and women." He looks around us then leans in closer as if he's revealing a secret. "Men keep their distance if they feel a woman is taken. Woman on the other hand accept it as a challenge." He grabs his phone. "I wouldn't doubt it if I had a text or call from her before we made it back to the apartment."

In the thrill of the dance floor I forgot to check my phone. I grab it from my purse and see several texts from Laila. "Speaking of texts, Laila is home." My smile grows wide. "Ready to get out of here?"

"Wow." Bryan grabs his chest. "Just like that you're done with me."

Putting my water glass on the bar, I link my arm with Bryan and walk toward the door. "Your words not mine." Darkness has settled and I shiver from the chill in the air. Brooklyn at night is different from Manhattan at night; the people on the streets look like they're at home. In Manhattan the people we passed looked like visitors. At the very least, they looked like commuters.

"Maybe you should have had that third drink." I look at Bryan through the side of my eyes. "You look too sober for this subway ride." He points up the street. "We aren't far from the apartment, thankfully. We'll take it a few stops up."

"Do all of your flings get a piece of art to commemorate the experience?" Bryan laughs. "That must be some serious dick. Needs to be memorialized."

He nudges my arm and says, "I don't like to brag." He wipes his hand over his beard. "I'm more of a show-and-tell type of guy." We stop at the bottom of the subway entrance. "Would you like a piece of my art?" My mouth drops but Bryan can't see my response. He's standing in front of me at the ticket machine. He turns around and hands me a card. "Was that a yes? Not sure I heard you." I grab the card from him and avoid his question.

Usually, I can go toe to toe with a guy, but the heat burning my cheeks is telling me otherwise. Maybe because I would like a piece of his art. Better yet, I want to know if his dick is worth memorizing. "What do we do now?"

"Scared?"

"The subway can't be that bad." Bryan smiles and shakes his head. He looks down and I follow his eyes. "Wait. What?" I look away from the bulge in his pants. I rub my hands together to resolve the moisture that's pooling there, but it's not doing a thing for the moisture between my thighs.

He laughs a hearty laugh then wraps his arm around my shoulder. "Let's take this subway ride before you rub your hands apart."

We step onto the train and the stench Bryan warned me about hits me and I can't control my gag reflex. I place my hand over my mouth and look to find a seat. Bryan tugs me toward an empty bench. "Only three stops before we get off." I close my eyes but Bryan nudges me until I squint at him. "You came for the experience." He points across from us at a sign marked with graffiti. "The only good thing about this space is the street art."

At the next stop a group of people step on the train. A guy who looks like he stepped out of the eighties stands in front of us in an Adidas tracksuit and matching Adidas shoes. Bryan points to my shoes and reminds me of my connection to the stranger. I shake my head and grab my neck. Unlike him I'm not rocking a big gold chain. Bryan whispers, "We're in New York. We can get you one of those on a street corner."

I try to laugh through my hand but fail, letting the piss

mixed with garbage smell invade my nose. "Think we could walk from the next stop?"

"We're on here now, we should just ride it out for one more." Bryan leans forward with his arms resting on his thighs and his face drawn into a scowl. Even with a scowl on his face he's sexy. I almost feel bad for making him endure this ride.

Bryan hops up and grabs my hand. He ushers me out of the train and up the subway stairs without stopping. When we are outside I move my hand and take a deep breath, thankful that the smell from the train is not embedded into my nose. "Next time I'll take you at your word."

Bryan reaches down wrapping his arms around me. I return his hug and ask, "What's that for?"

"It usually takes longer for me to persuade women to trust me." We walk away from the subway station and I'd be happy if that was the last time I ever saw it. "Too bad we are headed to the box with only one bathroom. I need to wash off that funk."

I rake my hands over my arms. "Yeah, we may have to flip to determine who goes first."

We stop in front of the apartment building that I would have overlooked had Bryan not slowed his pace. At night the facade is not recognizable and blends in seamlessly with the neighboring buildings. "Or we could just hop in together." Bryan grins but I can't separate his humor from truth.

Lightheartedly I say, "If we can get past Chris and Laila." He holds the door open for me and the woman exiting the building.

Bryan catches up with me before my finger presses the elevator call button. "Did you enjoy your tour around New York?" We step into the empty elevator car. "If not, your homegirl may kick me out." Just like that our banter is over. Guess it was humor.

"If art sales don't pick up before you run out of money you have a career as a guide." I look at him leaning against the elevator wall with his hands in his pockets. His eyes are watching me carefully, and I'm hoping these elevator doors open before I want to pounce on him. We stare at each other but I keep myself on my side of the elevator and he doesn't move.

"It'll be a humble life." We both watch as the elevator doors open and he says, "After you."

I walk to the apartment door, taking each step cautiously. Out front, my fist stills before the door. I want to see Laila, but I don't want my time with Bryan to end here. He hovers behind me and although he complained of smelling like hot garbage I can smell a faint woodsy, spicy scent that I'll always associate with him. Then I knock. Before I can no longer resist him, I knock again until Laila opens the door. I exhale. I didn't realize I was holding my breath until I was reminded I needed to breathe.

Laila wraps me in her arms and I yell, "Damn girl. I had told Chris I was coming for you if they didn't let you out of that place."

Laila laughs and whispers in my ear, "From the look of you two I don't think you cared one bit." I smile and release her from our embrace. I look around the apartment to search for Chris and she says, "He's in the room."

Bryan finds a seat on the couch and is swiping through his phone. "Laila, what do you have planned for your girl for the rest of the night?" He looks over to me. "I pretty much showed her all of the highlights of the city."

I nod in agreement. "Yes, he was a great tour guide." Laila walks toward the kitchen and pulls a bottle of Hennessy out of the cabinet followed by a bottle of coke.

"I was thinking we'd stay in tonight and catch up." She winces. "I have to work early in the morning." Before I can respond she puts her hand in the air to stop me. "But I won't be working all day."

"What exactly are you doing anyway?" I sit on a barstool in front of her. "Can't you write an article from just about anywhere?" When Laila graduated from L. U. she had an offer to work at *What's Happening Jacksonville?* where she would have stayed in Florida. Chris had different plans for her. He was moving to New York and got her an offer at *Millennial Magazine*.

She pours a few glasses of Hennessy, and handing me one, she says, "I can write from just about anywhere. But this weekend I'm working on a story with a team of people. We are up against a tight deadline and after the editor scrapped our first submission, we had to start from scratch mid-week."

Frowning I say, "Sounds tough. Much more complicated than my day job."

Bryan sits beside me. "Laila, are you hoarding all that for the two of you?" He points to the glasses.

Chris walks out of the room looking as if he just rolled over from a nap. With sleep lines imprinted on his face he looks to all of us and smiles. "Packed house tonight."

Laila passes each of them a glass. With her glass raised in the air she says, "To our humble beginnings. May they always remind us to work harder." We clank glasses and Chris takes Bryan to the living room to leave Laila and I alone to talk.

"How is your job going?" Instead of taking a seat beside me she hops onto the kitchen counter.

"Definitely not what I want to be doing with my life for long. Documentation and sitting in meetings most of the day. Reviewing manuals for comparison. Listening to old white guys try to humor me. It's for the birds."

"Your description almost put me to sleep. I'm sure it's hard for you to be bored all day. Although I have long hours, I like what I'm doing." She looks over to Bryan and Chris sitting in the living room. "How was your day?" she asks in a low whisper. Biting my lip I'm trying to conceal my smile, but Laila catches on quick and her mouth drops open. "Wait did y'all..."

"No," I yell louder than necessary.

She starts laughing and takes a sip of her drink. "Why not?" She looks around the apartment. "Chris and I can leave you alone for a bit."

Chapter Five
BRYAN

Chris raises his glass and says, "You told me you needed Henny to tell me what happened that day." I look to the kitchen and watch Nicole lean into Laila. Whispering in this matchbox apartment is necessary for the sake of privacy.

"Damn dude." Chris draws my attention back to him. "You feeling her?" As I shake my head, the reality of his question weighs on me. I can't remember the last time, if one existed, that I didn't just want to fuck a chick and keep it moving.

"That day was crazy." To avoid staring at Nicole I adjust myself and face Chris directly. From where I sit I can look out of the window, half the size of the wall, and see the Brooklyn Bridge. "You still haven't had the privilege to work with Dad in all his glory." Chris' eyes narrow as he listens. He's been Dad's golden child since birth. "At times I think he shielded you from his personality to ensure you stayed on board."

"And why he thinks I should be the one to carry the torch, I have no idea." Chris stares into his empty glass.

"We may need more of this before this story is over." But he doesn't move from his spot.

"Growing up David was the one who was the most interested in the business. Like Dad's protégé`. Until he wasn't anymore." Out of the three of us, David is the only one who truly wants to be in the business. He understands the market and has spent endless time learning the ins and outs of real estate. He even sacrificed a professional sports career to be in Tennessee. He's been ready and willing waiting on my dad to retire.

Chris wasn't old enough to understand that situation either. Being the youngest child affords you the opportunity to come in after some of the bullshit of life has already happened, and because it's bullshit, nobody rehashes the memories for your sake.

"That's another story for another day. I don't understand how David fell from Dad's good graces." Chris shakes his head. "Our family is more complicated than I thought." I nod my head in agreement.

"You know Mrs. Davenport, right?" I look at Chris to wait for his reaction and he looks up to the ceiling trying to recall his memory. "The Davenports, her husband was mayor when we were growing up." He looks at me with a smirk on his face. "Anyway. They were our clients." I stop and shake my head. "She was one of our clients." Chris shrugs his shoulders.

"Damn." He smiles slightly then says, "I think I know where this could be going."

"Yeah you can probably guess. She and her husband were separated, and she was actually working with us to sell one of their properties. She planned to move out of Tennessee." I look behind me to Nicole and her and Laila are still talking in a low whisper. "I love all women, but never had a thing for older women."

Chris laughs and looks at me. "How old is old?"

I smirk. "Older than Mom." I sigh realizing how bad that sounds. "Don't get me wrong Mrs. Davenport is one of those woman who has transcended time. If I saw her on the street and didn't know who she was I'd probably shoot my shot."

"Damn. Okay." Chris stands up and grabs my empty glass from my hand. "We need a refill." When Chris goes into the kitchen Laila engages him. She tells him how hungry she is and asks if he wants to grab something to eat. Nicole looks over her shoulder and our eyes meet.

Instead of either of us looking away we both stare until Laila interrupts us saying, "In a few we'll run out to get some food." She stretches her neck toward me. "You and Nicole can get comfortable and we'll bring y'all something back." Laila is far from dumb. I know what she's trying to do and I don't mind at all.

"We can let the guys stay here. You've ditched me all day." I'm surprised Nicole is denying herself a chance to stick around with me.

Chris looks over to me and his eyes grow wide. "I mean we could just order delivery and nobody has to leave." He walks back over to the couch handing me my drink. "Probably too late for you two to be out alone on these gritty New York streets."

Laila sighs in defeat. "Let me get my phone to find a restaurant that will deliver." She leaves the kitchen and Nicole doesn't look back at me.

"So Mrs. Davenport," Chris sips his drink. "The fine ass cougar."

I laugh and shake my head. An image of her body is embedded in my memory. The thought of her makes my dick shudder. "I knew she wanted me. What I didn't know is that she was just trying to get back at her husband. Using me as a pawn in her evil game of chess."

"Sounds like some serious shit."

"It was. At least in Dad's eyes. When her husband found out, he called Dad and asked 'What type of brothel are you running?' Punk ass." If he wasn't old we may have had it out, but I admit I shouldn't have banged his wife. Not like I pursued her though.

"So how'd dad know it was you? And what'd he say."

"Who else would be bold enough to bang Mrs. Davenport?" Chris and I both laugh. I look back to Nicole again. Although her back is toward me I can see her hand scrolling on her phone. Laila is in front of her doing the same. I assume they are looking for food options.

"On that day he called you into the office what happened?"

"I went into his office and he told me about his little conversation with Mr. Davenport. Told me I wouldn't make it in the company if I didn't put my dick aside." I tap my fingers together to indicate "blah blah blah." "Some other shit about me being a rebel."

Chris rolls his eyes. "And you just quit?"

"It wasn't just the fact that he had an issue with me fucking a bad bitch. It was that he told me I thought my art could sustain me and I didn't need the company." I looked back out the window to the Brooklyn Bridge. "That if I cared as much for the business as I did for my paintings I'd make it far." The grip on my glass tightens as I rekindle the feelings from that day. "The thing is the business was never for me. I dropped out of school because I realized art was a bigger part of me and I was neglecting it."

"Quitting and moving to New York to pursue your art career is like a fuck you to Dad, right?"

I smile because my brother's interpretation of the situation is spot on. "Exactly."

"You better make it in the art world. I'd hate to see what would happen if Dad had the opportunity to say 'I told you so'."

"It helped that Mrs. Davenport felt like shit for what happened."

Chris' eyes bulge. "For real?"

"Yup. She commissioned a piece and convinced her friends to do the same."

"And because I'm no fool I made sure they paid a pretty penny for those pieces." I laugh, remembering each of the women being excited to receive their art. "I even heard from one of them that the piece I sold Mrs. Davenport hung proudly in her master bedroom. Her husband had no clue what he saw each and every day."

"Yeah? What was the piece you sold her called?"

I rub the stubble growing outside of my goatee. "Loveless marriage."

"Wow." Chris pats my shoulder. "Sounds like a checkmate to me."

"Food should be here in a few minutes," Laila shouts from the kitchen.

Chris and I walk into the kitchen and ask, "What did you order?"

Nicole looks at Laila with a coy smile that makes my dick shudder again. "Chinese."

"What's that smile for?" I ask.

"I want to have a full New York experience, including cheap Chinese food from a sketchy restaurant."

I look at Laila and say, "Being around your friend should come with hazard duty pay." Laila looks up at me and cocks her head. "Riding the subway, eating sketchy food. She's determined to kill me."

We all laugh and then Laila breaks up the fun by telling us that she has to work again in the morning. "One day you won't have to work so hard." Chris pulls Laila into his chest wrapping his arms around her neck. "One day I'll come home and tell you to quit your job."

Laila leans back and says, "But it's the job you got for me."

"Right. We'll have something of our own one day." Nicole and I sigh simultaneously. Chris looks to me and says, "Don't hate because you don't want to settle down."

My eyes turn toward Nicole and she looks away. "Whatever dude. Save that mushy stuff for the bedroom." I pass him my glass. "In the meantime fill 'er up."

A loud knock bellows at the door and Laila says, "Food is here."

"We just skipped our plan to get clean after our trip on the subway." I stretch my arm out and wave it across my chest. "Just spreading funk all over their place."

Nicole smiles and says, "You're right." She sniffs her shirt. "Either the liquor is distorting my senses or it wore off already."

Laila places the bags on the counter. "At least wash your hands." She pulls out the food, examining each container before laying it open on the counter. "Then let's dig in."

While we eat, Chris fills us in on the progress of the expansion here in New York. He's taken our firm, which was doing great in Tennessee, and rebuilt the brand for the market here in New York. As I watch him discuss future plans with enthusiasm I understand why my dad has pegged him as the golden child. "You almost make me believe this is what you want to be doing."

"If I can't do what I love, I should love what I do." Chris winks at Laila, soliciting another sigh from both Nicole and I.

I shake my head. "If you get this thing off the ground here, you can hire people to handle the details. With you overseeing, you'll have time to pick up something else."

I lean back and grab my stomach. The grease from the Chinese food has settled and the mixture with the

Hennessy is not helping it digest. "Hazard duty pay," I say looking at Nicole.

"You didn't like this food?" She says as she stuffs another forkful into her mouth.

"It's not that I don't like the food, but the food doesn't like me." I put my fork down and stand up, taking my plate to the kitchen. The apartment isn't large enough for a dining table. Instead, we sit around the coffee table in the living room, legs stretched in front of us because our ability to sit legs crossed failed, at least for Chris and I, though Laila and Nicole are sitting, legs crossed, with ease.

Laila follows me into the kitchen, putting her plate in the sink. She yawns then declares, "I need to get to bed before dawn is upon us."

"What? You aren't an early bird anymore?" Nicole says from the living room.

Laila shakes her head vigorously. "No, you ladies killed that for me in school."

Chris follows Laila into the bedroom, leaving Nicole with me. Laila throws a blanket out to Nicole and the both of us look at the couch with skepticism.

"Wait. The funk may have worn off, but there's no way I'm sleeping in these clothes. I need a shower." She grabs her bag and knocks on the bedroom door. I'm tempted to join her. Would get us out of their bedroom sooner. Laila does have to work in the morning. I scan the room for my bag but decide against it. I'd hate for her to reject my idea.

Instead I sit on the chair with my head rested on the back.

"Bryan." She nudges my shoulder. "You can go next."

I open my eyes slowly and find Nicole in front of me in the skimpiest of pajamas. As my eyes adjust to being open, I blink and I'm pleasantly surprised when my focus narrows in on her breasts, her nipples standing at attention. She turns away before I can fully enjoy them.

"Thanks. Your shower must have been long. Didn't realize I was that tired."

She grabs the blanket and stretches out across the couch fluffing the blanket over herself. "I'm exhausted." She looks back to me and says in a gentle whisper, "Thanks again for today." Through a yawn she continues, "I enjoyed myself." I grab my bag and leave her to rest.

Chapter Six
NICOLE

My phone dings with a text message.
Laila: Breakfast in the kitchen. I'll be back by lunch.
Stretching over my head my shirt reveals my nipple and I cover it before anyone can see. Then I search for the person I expected to be stretched out nearby. Bryan. Where's Bryan?

A beep from the kitchen draws my attention and I see Chris opening the microwave. "Good morning," he says with a groggy voice.

"Good morning." I slip from under the covers and walk toward him. "Don't tell me you have to work today too?"

He looks down at his clothes. "No, I wear suits to the gym." He laughs. His gray suit with a subtle yellow tie fits him well. "Sorry. Too early in the morning."

"No problem. If it weren't so early, I'd have a nice comeback for you but I need coffee." He points to a container on the counter.

"Guess the hospitality wore off last night," I say as I round the counter and grab the container.

"You guessed right. You are no longer a guest in our

humble abode. You are family. Help yourself to anything you need." He grabs his keys from the counter. "I'll be back in a couple of hours."

Before the door closes behind him I shout, "Hey where's Bryan?"

He peeks his head back into the doorway and says, "He wanted to give you space to sleep. Not sure where he went though."

I finish making my cup of coffee and with a handful of grapes I return to my makeshift bed. Scrolling through my news collection from my social media accounts I think about Bryan's offer to get me laid for the weekend. It's not a bad idea. It'd be better if he were offering.

The knock at the door startles me. I ignore the first couple of knocks because clearly this isn't my place and neither of the residents are here. They also didn't mention they expected visitors, or a package, or a delivery of some sort. The doorknob jiggles and I still my breathing. Maybe they heard me and know I'm in here. Shit. I walk to the kitchen and grab the empty bottle of Hennessy.

On my tippy toes I look through the peep whole then snatch the door open. With the bottle at my side I say, "You almost got knocked out."

Bryan laughs and walks past me, placing bags on the counter. "Good thing I didn't use my key."

Next to his bag, I sit the empty bottle down. I raise my eyebrow at him as I walk back to my seat and grab my phone. I'd love to know where he went last night. Love to ask a million questions about why he didn't stay, but that's not my place.

"Did you sleep well last night?" He says as he ruffles the bag on the counter.

"As well as one could on a couch." I look over at him in the kitchen. "The liquor probably helped. But I'm not sure how you've been sleeping on this thing for the past few weeks."

"Right. Exactly why I'm looking for a place today." He walks over to the couch and hands me a container. "Did Laila mention my apartment hunt she volunteered you for?" I open the container and the smell of eggs and bacon makes me smile. Much better than the few grapes I just had.

"Thanks for the food." Moving the covers to my side of the couch he sits beside me with his own container. After a bite I say, "She didn't mention it."

"I volunteered her, then she bowed out because of work and passed to you." I shrug. "You don't mind?"

"Nope." He looks down at my clothes and I say, "After I finish eating I'll get changed."

He laughs. "You can wear that sheer shirt if you want." He swallows a bite of food and continues, "I may be distracted all day though."

Following his eyes I realize my nipples are perfectly perky and giving him a full show. "I'm sure you've seen plenty of nipples before."

He chokes on his food and puts his hand up. I pat his back until his coughing subsides. "I could see all the nipples the world has to offer and still get excited by them."

I shake my head and roll my eyes. Taking another bite of my toast I close the box and stand up. Crossing in front of him I grab my bag and walk toward the bedroom. Behind me I hear him say, "Let me know if you need help. I can get those hard to reach places for you." As much as I would love to fuck him in the shower, or on that couch, I resist and close the door behind me.

Rummaging through my luggage, I finally find an outfit that matches the occasion. While packing for the trip, I didn't plan for many sophisticated events. I imagined me and Laila exploring the nooks and crannies of the city, eating at small restaurants with big followings, dancing at a low-key lounge, people watching in Central Park. Although that would have been my idea of a perfect weekend, the alternative is beginning to redefine my meaning of perfect.

"Ready to roll?" I ask Bryan as I step out of Laila's room.

With his head down he responds with a barely audible, "Yup." He slides his phone into his pocket then stands up from the couch. When he finally looks up at me his eyebrows arch and he says, "Wow."

I look down at my dress snug around my chest but flowing loosely from my waist to just above my knee. When I bought it, the yellow flowers caught my eye. I don't usually pick up blue clothes but from the look on Bryan's face I'm glad I grabbed this one from the mall. I shrug and say, "Too much for apartment hunting?" Bryan looks at me without responding. "It's either this or festival wear."

"Festival wear?" He asks with his eyebrows knitted together.

"Yeah cut-off shorts and a tank top." I laugh then walk to the door. With my hand on the knob I say, "Not sure it'd fit the grown man vibe you are on today."

Close behind me I hear him chuckle. When we reach the elevator, I reach for the down button but Bryan reaches around me and presses the up button. I turn to him and squint my eyes. The elevator doors open and we step in to ride the elevator up a few floors. When we step off Bryan checks his phone before guiding us to a door.

As we wait for someone to answer his knocks I lean against the wall beside the door. "Like this building enough to stay?" Bryan's smile returns sending my hormones into overdrive.

"My brother has good taste," he responds as the door swings open.

"Come on in." The apartment manager steps aside, inviting us in with a wave of her hand. With her hand outstretched, she introduces herself and shakes both of our hands.

"Nice to meet you, Zya," Bryan says while looking toward me. "And thank you for the last minute appointment. Like I said, I wanted my girlfriend to see the place before she goes back South tomorrow."

Zya looks at me with admiration and it takes all my willpower to remain un-phased by the introduction and Bryan's ease at feeding her the lie. Instead I say, "Yes, I'll feel more comfortable leaving if I know where he'll be resting his head."

"Take your time and look around. I'll be here if you have any questions." Bryan grabs my hand and we walk out of Zya's sight. The apartment's floor plan is similar to Chris and Laila's apartment. The view of the Brooklyn Bridge is available through the large windows and although I admired it in great detail from Laila's apartment, it draws me in and I stop in front of the windows to stare.

"Beauty fit for a canvas," Bryan says. I nod in agreement. "Let's check out the bedroom." Bryan grabs my hand and I follow closely behind him.

"Not much different from downstairs." I walk toward the bathroom. "What other places do you plan on looking at today?"

"I think I'm sold actually." I jump in response to Bryan's proximity. "Did I scare you?"

"I didn't realize you were right behind me." I look into the mirror and watch as he stands over my shoulder. My heart begins to race and I walk away, leaving him in the bathroom.

"What do you think?" Zya says from the doorway of the bedroom.

I turn to Bryan and wait for him to respond. "Up to you babe," I say with a smirk.

"I think we'll take it." He walks over to me and kisses my cheek. The spot turning warm after his lips leave it. Turning to Zya with his hand outstretched he asks, "Is it possible to get the keys tonight?"

Zya and I both exchange looks and she nods cautiously before answering, "That may be possible."

"Great, what time should I come down to pick them up?" Zya confirms a time and we leave the apartment. On our way to the elevator Bryan asks, "Think I could bother you for a few more hours?"

With my hand on my hip I say, "Not like Laila will be home soon. What do you have in mind?"

"I need to pick out a bed." Thinking about Bryan in a bed sends a tingle up my spine and I adjust my feet before nodding my head and agreeing to tag along with him to find a bed. When the elevator opens, we step in, and I'm thankful for the folks riding with us. Being alone with him on another ride could be detrimental to my resolve.

Before we reach the lobby, my phone vibrates and I answer the call. "Laila, are you finally off?" I look up to catch Bryan press the button for Laila's floor.

"Yes," she shouts into the phone. "I'm actually already at the apartment. Where are you?"

The question makes me squirm and I whisper, "I came with Bryan to look at an apartment."

"Oh," she says sounding deflated. "No rush, I'll be here when you return."

"No, it's cool. You caught us as we were about to go out furniture shopping. I'll just come back to the apartment." As the elevator opens we exit and walk down the hallway.

I look at Bryan and apologize. He's filled in when Laila

left me hanging and I feel obligated to repay him, but he says, "It's cool. You are here to see Laila. I'm glad she's finally off from work. I'll go find a bed and see if I can persuade them to deliver it today." He wiggles his eyebrows. "I'd rather sleep in a bed than on a blow up mattress."

"Yeah I'm sure either will beat the comfort of their couch." I knock on the door and before I can move my hand the door swings open.

Laila wraps Bryan in a hug and says, "Thanks for entertaining Nicole. You're the best brother of a boyfriend a girl could have."

He laughs and says, "You can call me brother-in-law." Bryan releases Laila and looks beyond her into the apartment. "But since you're taking your bestie back, I need Chris to come with me furniture shopping." He stretches his neck. "Where is he?"

Chris appears from the bedroom and says, "Did I hear you say furniture shopping?" Bryan nods his head. "Does that mean you found a place and we can have ours back?" He wraps his arm around Laila's waist as he waits for Bryan to respond. I smile at Laila and the look on her face is sincere. After all the two of them have been through, I'm happy they are back together.

"You aren't getting rid of me entirely," Bryan says. "I'll be a few floors above you."

"As long as it's not in this space, I'm good," Chris says. He walks toward the bedroom while saying, "Let me grab my shoes and I'll come furniture shopping with you."

Laila claps her hands with excitement. "That leaves the two of us. There's still time for us to catch the food truck festival." Chris and Laila grab their things and we exit the building together, going our separate ways when we hit the street, Chris and Bryan leaving in a taxi and Laila and I on foot.

Alone for the first time, Laila turns to me and says, "I hope you won't hold this weekend against me."

"Like never plan another trip to New York to visit you or be too busy for you to visit me in Atlanta?" I laugh then say, "Hasn't crossed my mind. Not even once."

Laila taps my arm and says, "I deserve that." As we continue for another couple of blocks she gives me more details about the article for the magazine, although I'll read it next month when it's released, I've been a subscriber since she started at *Millennial Magazine*.

While she continues talking I begin thinking about my time with Bryan, and how I felt when he was in my personal space, how his warm lips made me feel more excited than I've felt with other guys who were doing much more than a kiss to my cheek. But how it all seems to be a game for him, a game I'm not willing to risk my heart to play. Besides, he's already expressed his interest in getting me a dude this weekend, which I can only assume means he doesn't want to be the dude.

Laila's arm crosses my face as she points in the direction of a parking lot. "That's the food truck festival. Let's cross the street here."

When we reach the ticket booth we both dig in our purses for the ten-dollar fee, but Laila swats at my hand when I try to hand my money to the attendant. "My treat for skipping out on you." We walk past the ticket booth and into a swarm of people wrapped in long lines in front of each of the food trucks.

"There are too many options," I say with a frown. "Where should we start?"

"The Jamaican beef patties can't be a bad first start." I follow Laila to the Jamaican food truck and we stand in the never-ending line. "So…" Laila nudges me in the side and I already know where this conversation is going. Laila has never been the subtle one, always in somebody's business. "Do you like Bryan?"

I roll my eyes at her and say, "He's cute." I turn my head toward the menu on the truck.

"What?" She stands in front of me, blocking my view of the menu. "That's it? He's cute."

With a smirk I ask, "What else do you want to know?"

"He seems like he likes you."

"Bryan?" I shake my head. "I'd find it hard to believe there's a woman alive he doesn't like."

"Think you'll ever settle down?" Laila is the relationship type. She's had a few long-term relationships, and had a difficult time being single and dating multiple guys.

"If I found a guy like Chris or Josh even." My smile tightens. "Josh minus the cheating." Josh is Laila's best friend's brother, and when we first met I was all over him. Then I realized he only had eyes for Laila and I gave up hope. When Josh and Laila dated, I was a little jealous. I had a close-up of the type of guy he was, the type of love he was capable of giving. He adored everything about Laila, but just couldn't compete with Chris.

When he cheated on her I was probably as heartbroken as her. Not only because she's my friend and she was hurting, but because he was an ideal guy, a guy I thought could do no wrong. When he did, my theory of fucking and leaving was solidified.

"It'll happen." Laila wraps her arm around my shoulder. "And maybe Bryan is the guy who could change everything for you."

Chapter Seven
BRYAN

"Damn, Bryan, you better be glad you're my brother." Chris drags his feet through the store. "I can think of better ways to be spending my Saturday afternoon."

I look at him and laugh. "I thought you would be happy. I'm getting out of your space."

He taps my shoulder and says, "Bryan, happy doesn't even begin to express my feelings about you getting out of our space." I touch my chest and act hurt although I understand his sentiment. "Not that I don't love you, but the place is barely big enough for us."

"Yeah this New York living is different from down south." My condo in Tennessee is spacious. Having a few guests is hardly noticeable.

"Think you'll go back home?" I've always been spontaneous, but moving to New York was the most random thing I've done. Ever. I didn't think through a plan, hence me crashing on Chris' couch for weeks. I want to make this art thing work, and New York seems the most plausible place for that to happen. But if it doesn't, I don't know what's next.

"We'll see what happens. What about you?" If it were up to our dad, Chris would already be home. Not sure how long he can avoid him.

"Not if it's up to me." Chris sits down on a couch and smooths the leather with his hand. "Are you only looking for a bed today?"

"Yeah that's my first priority."

Chris laughs and shakes his head. "So the chicks you have over will have no choice but to be in your bed." He laughs harder but stops laughing when he realizes I'm not joining him.

"Whatever man. After sleeping on your couch for weeks. I would be happy to not see a couch for a while." Chris nods his head. I walk away from him as a store attendant asks me if I need assistance.

"If I make a purchase today, could you have it delivered this evening?" The store attendant's eyes widen.

"We have a few items in stock in the warehouse. If it's something you like we could make a special arrangement to have it delivered this evening." By special arrangement, I assume he means with a hefty cost, but at this point I don't even care.

"I need a bed. Show me what you have." We walk over to the few beds they have in stock and only one fits my style. We complete the sale and I walk over to Chris and tell him how helpless he's been. "We can leave now."

He hops off the couch and says, "Good. Now let's find something to get into." Instead of taking a taxi back to the apartment, we walk until we find a restaurant to pop into.

Sitting across from each other, we get comfortable and I drill Chris about his plans with Laila. "I mean when are you going to marry her?" After Chris made the grand gesture of finding Laila a job at *Millennial Magazine*, and convincing her to move to New York instead of Jacksonville where she had a job offer, you'd think they'd be running down the aisle.

He wipes at his nose. "No rush. We'll get there." I'm sure he has something else in mind. He's never been able to hide his tell of wiping at his nose. I just smirk and don't badger him any further about their relationship. "Besides, I'm the youngest. You and David need to lead the way."

We both laugh, knowing how hard it would be to get us both married off before him. "Nice try, bro, not happening anytime soon. At least not for me." I look across the restaurant to a group of ladies sitting at a booth. "I like my freedom to roam." I look back to Chris who is now looking at the group of ladies.

"One of us better get married before Mom starts nagging," Chris groans. Our mother, fortunate to have three stubborn boys, has latched on to any female we've ever brought home. In recent years, I've had random girls come and go and my mom's attention to the chicks was apprehensive. But I saw how she was with Laila. It was like she had already accepted her as a daughter, more concerned for her well-being and feelings than for Chris'.

"Yeah go ahead and take that one for the team. And while you're at it give her a grand-kid and I'll have years before she starts looking at me expecting me to settle down."

After a couple of drinks and wings we decide to continue on our walk back to the apartment. Chris wanted to check in with the ladies before we made plans for the night, a gentle reminder that I wasn't ready to settle down yet. I, on the other hand, was ready to hit a club or a bar, and hadn't thought twice about Laila and Nicole. Maybe about Nicole, just about those curves, and maybe her wit. Not too many women can keep up with my sense of humor.

When we walk into Chris' apartment we find the two of

them laid out in the living room. "How was the food truck festival?" Chris asks Laila.

Laila rubs her stomach and says, "I think we tried just about everything out there." She looks over at Nicole who is frozen on the floor. "Probably not the best idea to mix all that food."

Nicole groans.

I sit down next to Nicole and say, "You're determined to have the shits on your flight home, huh?" Nicole rolls her eyes at me. The pathetic look on her face made me feel bad for her. "Need some medicine?" Without moving her head, she looks at me with a pathetic smile. I stand up and offer to go to the corner store for medicine.

On my way to the door I hear Chris ask Laila, "Are you two going to be able to go out tonight or are you all in?"

"We're waiting on Nicole's boo to text her. She may have plans of her own." I turn and look at Laila who has a wide grin on her face and I open the door and walk out of the apartment.

Unlike Tennessee, I can walk just about anywhere near the apartment. The corner store is just a few feet from the entrance. From the shelf, I grab a bottle of Pepto-Bismol and try to check my feelings. Something about Nicole having plans with a dude tonight makes me uncomfortable. I try to make myself believe it's because I haven't had the chance to have her for myself. But that's never phased me before. If a girl was taken, I usually move on to the next without a problem, many times, the next being her homegirl.

Laila and Nicole are still in the same spot in the living room when I walk through the door. I hand Nicole the medicine then call for Chris. "We headed out tonight or what?" I ask when he peeps his head through the bedroom door. "These two look like they are all in for the night."

Chris looks at Laila then shrugs his shoulders. "I'm

down." We agree we'll head out later that night and I leave the trio to go get my bed set up in my apartment.

The sterile feeling of the apartment evades me. Earlier when Zya and Nicole joined me, the apartment didn't feel as empty and I hardly noticed the echoes caused from our movement in the open space.

Although I don't want to see a couch anytime soon, I will need to finish furnishing the place this week. But the walls, those will remain empty until I can return from Tennessee with my pieces.

Leaning against the kitchen counter, I visualize each wall of the apartment filled with the bountiful colors and soft strokes of my canvases. Now that I've found an apartment I need to find an art studio. A knock at the door interrupts my thoughts.

Through the peephole I see what appears to be a deliveryman. "Bryan," he says through the door.

"That's me," I say after opening the door. He presents the delivery slip and I show him where I want the bed set up. After they finish the setup they drop a few more bags and I look at them questioning the contents. "What's this?"

"Guess you made a friend of the manager. She wanted you to have sheets and a comforter and hopes you'll be back for your other furniture needs in the future." The guy smirks after he delivers the message as if he had memorized it and was proud he hadn't messed up the words.

"I'll definitely be back." Customer service is my soft spot. I'll probably furnish my entire apartment from her store now. As the deliverymen leave the apartment I consider a possible partnership with the furniture store. I could make affordable pieces for her to sell. I tuck that idea away and finish setting up the bed.

My phone dings, notifying me of a text message. I can hear the phone but can't find it. The apartment is empty and doesn't take long to look in the obvious places, but I can't find my phone in my bedroom or in my kitchen. Whoever it is looking for me will hopefully call if they really need me, and then I'll be able to find it.

I finish making up my bed when I hear a knock at my door. I look out of the peephole and see Nicole standing with her hand on her hip.

Pushing the door open she grins at me and says, "I was starting to think you already had company." She looks past me through the door and asks, "Do you?"

Pulling her arm into the door I say, "I just finished making my bed." I look behind me to the bedroom. "Now, I can invite a few chicks over." We both laugh and she leans against the kitchen counter. "Still feeling that shady food from earlier or did the medicine help?"

"It helped. Thanks again." She pats her stomach. "I think I'll stick with decent food till I leave." I cock my eyebrow at her and smirk. "Your brother was calling to tell you we were tagging along but you didn't answer the phone, and because I couldn't remember your apartment number to send him to tell you in person." She points to her chest. "I was volunteered to come up here."

"Maybe you can help me find my phone while you're here." She looks around the apartment without moving. "If you pull out your phone we can call it."

She laughs and reaches into her back pocket to hand me her phone. After entering my number into her phone, I save it with Big Daddy stored as the name. I dial my number and hand it back to her while I listen for my phone to ring.

"Big Daddy," she says as she follows behind me.

With my phone ringing in the background I say, "I knew that would sound orgasmic coming out of your mouth." All day Nicole has been able to go toe to toe with me, even keeping a straight face when I kissed her cheek and convinced Zya that we were in a relationship. But her audible gasp just now proves that she's embarrassed or I caught her off guard.

"I think it's under the bed." I turn to look at her and her eyes are set on my bed. "Your phone." She points toward my bed.

Kneeling down, I rake my hand under the bed and my hand lands on my phone. With it raised in the air I say, "You're right." She hangs up her phone.

Looking around the room she says, "I'm going back downstairs to get dressed." I close the gap between us and invade her personal space. Her breath catches when she turns back toward me. "Ugh." She coughs to clear her throat. "See you in a bit?"

Reaching out to her waist I let my hand rest above her hip. "Actually, I need to raid Chris' place for some necessities until I get this place set up." With my eyebrows arched I say, "You're more than welcome to get dressed here. I'll grab towels for you too."

"Actually, that may not be a bad idea. At least I won't have to wait long for the shower." This time it was my turn to be caught off guard.

Chapter Eight
NICOLE

My phone dings with a text message.
Laila: Did you just ditch me?
Laila: And you sent Bryan to tell me?
My laughter echoes through Bryan's empty apartment. I don't know if I want to cross that line with Bryan, considering it won't be a love him and leave him situation. For as long as Laila and Chris are together, Bryan will be around.
And why all of a sudden is he interested in me? Initially, he was all for helping me find someone to dick me down before I left the city. Now, he seems like he wants to take that task on himself.
Nicole: Girl, I'm just going to get dressed up here so we can all get ready quicker.
I put my phone down because I'm sure Laila will fire off a slew of messages. But she'll be okay. The front door opens and Bryan walks in carrying my luggage, towels and random clothes. "You'll have to find a better way to move your things from downstairs."
He hunches his shoulders and looks around the apartment before sitting everything on the floor in front of the

door. "I only had a few bags when I moved here. I just need to work on getting the apartment set up." He rubs the back of his neck. "It's been a while since I started from scratch." Another reminder of our age gap.

"Your girl was a little upset that you didn't come back downstairs," he says as he walks toward me with my luggage in his hand. "We should make this betrayal worthwhile." I cock my head at him and raise my eyebrow. "Take a shower with me."

Before I can respond my head is shaking no. "I need to figure out what I'm wearing. You can go ahead and I'll hop in after you."

He shrugs his shirt over his shoulders and says, "If that's what you want." The art covering his back causes me to watch him walk away. Instead of rummaging through my luggage I follow him to the bathroom where the door is conveniently open wide enough for me to see him standing in front of the mirror.

I knock lightly on the door and Bryan looks up and says, "You don't have to knock. I invited you in."

I open the door wider and ask, "What's the art on your back?"

He turns away from me giving me an unfettered view of the full piece. Then he explains, "It's an African collage." As he describes each image encased in the shell of the continent, I locate the image on his back: an elephant, lion, shackled wrists, and a Marula Tree.

Before he finishes his description, my hand reaches out and traces each of the images. "It's breath-taking. So elaborate." He turns to face me and grabs my hand, placing it on the art covering his chest.

"Thank you." He looks down at his chest and says, "For years I used my body as my creative outlet." He laughs before saying, "My mom suggested I start on canvas before my whole body was covered."

He drops my hand then scoots my shirt off my shoulder and asks, "What about you? Are you hiding any art?"

I laugh at the thought. I point to myself and say, "Me? Getting a tattoo? I had to draw the line with my rebellion. My pastor father would have had a fit if I came home with a tattoo. I'd never hear the end of it." Just as if it had happened I can imagine my father fussing at me about my body being a sacred temple.

"Probably for the best. They are a bit addictive." I'd heard this before from a few friends who started with one tattoo and a few later were still thinking about what they would get next.

I look at the shower then remember we are supposed to be getting ready for the club. "I'm slowing us down. I still haven't found an outfit for tonight."

He points to the door and says, "Yeah get out of here before you see all my art on display." He looks down at his crotch and I realize the piece of art he is referring to is not one he crafted himself. I back out of the door with my gaze stuck on what could probably be His greatest masterpiece.

The shower starts once I'm safely out of the bathroom and I'm thankful he didn't undress anytime sooner because I'm slowly losing my ability to stay away. My ability to ignore my pulsating sex and hard nipples is damn near impossible. Instead of giving in to my desires I return to my suitcase and find an outfit that would be sure to help me curve my sexual tensions, and help me find a man willing to break my back, no questions asked, before I leave the city tomorrow.

"You're up next," Bryan says. I look up from my suitcase. "I put towels in the bathroom for you." He says this as his towel hangs low on his waist and beads of water are still dripping down his chest.

I grab my outfit and slide past him to the bathroom. Over the spray of water, I can hear music coming from the bedroom. I can't make out the words but the beat sounds familiar.

I peek my head out of the bathroom before stepping out. Bryan is dancing across his room buttoning his shirt. When he turns away I step out behind him and sway along with him to the music. Finally I hear the words of the song, *Cause I need somebody who will stand by me.* Bryan belts out the words, "Sunny days, everybody loves them."

I sing along with him and when he hears me, he turns around and wraps his arms around my waist and we sway to the song. When the words stop, he leans into me, connecting our lips. I don't pull away, I lean in, all the way in. I rub my hand across his chest where I know a tattoo rests beneath his shirt.

When the beat ends, we pull away, and I'm breathless. My eyes remain closed until I hear him ask, "Aren't you too young to be a New Edition fan?"

Leaning against his dresser I say, "We're all New Edition fans now thanks to the BET movie."

Bryan's head tilts back and laughter bellows out. "Yeah that movie did revive my love for their music. When I was a kid I used to try to learn all their dance moves. Even had Chris and David do the dances with me." Imagining the three of them in front of the television has me balled over in a fit of laughter.

I'm interrupted by Bryan's ringing phone. He looks down at it and says, "That's Chris, probably checking for us." He answers and tells him we'll be down shortly. Brushing against my skin, through my side cut outs, Bryan sings, "Candy girl," before walking out of his room.

With my clutch in hand I follow closely behind him and say, "With that voice *The Clark Brothers* could have been my favorite boy group growing up."

Bryan looks at me and shakes his head. "I assume you don't realize that was a group." He looks at me knowingly as he presses the elevator call button. With my eyes squinted I shake my head. He wraps his arm around my waist leading me into the open elevator. "So much to teach you youngin'."

"Remind me not to send your hot ass to send a message to a dude ever again." Laila grips my shoulder, pulling me into the apartment and away from Bryan.

"I'm ready," Chris yells from the bedroom.

Laila sits me on the couch and looks me square in the face. "What were y'all doing up there?" I look from her to Bryan standing in the kitchen. "Oh now you can't kiss and tell?" I feel my cheeks begin to burn when Bryan looks at me grinning. Laila acts as if her place isn't the size of a box and her voice isn't echoing throughout the apartment.

Through gritted teeth I say, "You're so embarrassing." There aren't many details to give her. As quickly as the kiss happened it was over as if it never happened. Not that Bryan and I needed to discuss what transpired or how our friendly banter escalated to a passionate kiss, a kiss that made me instantly want to wrap my legs around his waist and ride him into the night. Or how he went from my hoe matchmaker to my match. Those were all details that didn't matter much because it wouldn't happen again. He'll be back on his job at the club, with me pretending to be his sister, and him helping me find my next dude to fuck.

"Do you plan on going back there after the club?" Laila looks down at my clutch. "You didn't even bring your bags back. Just remember you have an early flight in the morning." She stands up, walks toward her bedroom and shouts, "Thought you were ready like ten minutes ago."

Watching me, Bryan answers Laila, "He always takes his time. Would have certainly thought he would have been a pretty boy Kappa instead of a nasty Que."

Chris emerges from the room and says, "Watch it." He

grabs his keys and Laila's hand. Over his shoulder he says, "Let's ride."

My feet rejoice when we are seated at the VIP table. My get 'em girl outfit would not have been complete without these six-inch heels. But after wearing tennis shoes for most of the weekend my feet aren't ready for the gentle assault the elevation inflicts on my arch.

"Let's take a shot," Laila hollers over the thump of the beat. After I throw the shot back Laila stands up and waves her hand toward me. "We're going to the dance floor." It's been a while since we've been in a club together, but the liquid courage must be something serious because Laila was the least coordinated dancer of all the roommates.

When we hit the dance floor we mix in with the dancers already moving to the music. The dance floor is much different from our years at L. U. where friends came with coordinated dances and chicks danced till they sweat their hair and outfits out. "Think Jennifer would like this up North music?" Laila shakes her head. We semi two-step through a few songs, nothing like the fast-paced booty-shaking we'd do down South. But before long my feet are begging for a break. "Let's sit down for a few."

"Yeah my feet are killing me." We both smile knowing we are on the same page. When we get back to the table, a few chicks are standing around talking to Chris and Bryan. When Chris notices us approaching, he scoots over and lets Laila sit beside him. He ignores the girls and starts whispering in Laila's ear. I scoot in beside Laila, giving Bryan his space to continue his conversation with the girls, just waiting on my opportunity to swoop in as his sister. He surprises me when he bids the chicks farewell and turns his attention to me.

"Not worthy of your artwork," I say sarcastically.

"Not even. I can't get my current muse off my mind."

He drapes his arm across the back of the seat and scoots in close to me.

"Is that right?" He nods his head and runs his hand over my knee.

"Her natural hair, brown eyes that hold an ocean of hope, an elongated neck," Bryan stares at me as if he were committing my face to memory. "Breasts that could feed a nation of children." I gasp and he laughs in response.

Chris looks at us and his eyes don't leave Bryan's hand on my knee. Bryan whispers, "Come home with me when we leave."

Chapter Nine
BRYAN

Whether alone or with a group of guys, the club has always been my zone to find women. Being able to pick up women who don't realistically expect an emotional attachment; women who are looking to relieve their woes, whatever they may be.

But tonight, tonight was different; the only woman I was interested in taking home was the one who came with me. Another first, not bringing sand to the beach was not only cliché` but it was my gold standard. And this weekend Nicole had me caught up twice.

Chris warned me, and Nicole ignored me, but I couldn't resist. Then that kiss. That kiss was hard to pull away from. If it weren't for our plans for the night I would have convinced her to stay in with me, to allow me to explore her body.

After the chicks in the club approached us and my dick didn't even flinch, I was assured I wanted Nicole. And I wanted her badly. If it were up to me, we would have exited stage left as soon as she came back to the table. I didn't want her liquored up, I wanted her sober, and fully aware of the passion I wanted to unleash on her.

I also didn't want to heed my luck to any other random dude who could have tried his hand with her. I knew her goal for the night. She just wanted to be fucked; at this point any old dude would do.

But she didn't respond when I asked her to come home with me. Standing across from her and Laila in the elevator I keep my eyes on the numbers as we are rising. Chris is trying to talk to me but I can't focus on his words. His floor is next, when the doors open my eyes connect with hers and I wait. Chris steps around me and takes Laila by the hand as they exit the elevator.

Nicole looks away from me as the doors begin to close. As the elevator starts to transcend we are alone. When the doors open at my floor I look to her. She steps off the elevator and leads the way to my apartment.

When I open the door I feel rushed, but I want to take my time with her. I take her purse and lay it on the counter then guide her to the bedroom, leading her by the waist. Chris was right, without a couch the only suitable option in here is the bed to sit.

I brush her hair behind her ear and break our silence, "I want you so bad right..." Our lips collide and she pushes me against the bed, her urgency obvious. I let her take lead, kissing me and climbing on top of me. I reach down to remove her shoes and then break from our kiss. "I don't want a quick fuck," I say.

She rocks back on her heels and concentrates on me. "That's all either of us is capable of doing." She shakes her head and continues, "We only have tonight. The few hours left of it."

"We owe ourselves more." I grab her behind the head and kiss her with every ounce of certainty I have within me.

My body tenses when I don't feel her relax. I release her from the kiss and ask, "Do you honestly believe you aren't capable of more than fucking and leaving?" She looks down and I say, "As a matter of fact, let's prove it to ourselves."

"Like not having sex at all?" She asks. "Leave me hot and heavy then send me home tomorrow with the thoughts of those kisses? And that's it?" She stands as if she is going to walk away.

"Don't leave. Take a shower with me." I reach for her and she doesn't move. "Listen, this is new to me too. I don't even know why I'm doing this. I'd love to be inside of you right now. But to be honest, I've enjoyed my time with you."

Nicole interrupts my outpouring. "You don't have to feed me all of that to fuck." She rolls her eyes. "I've heard every sweet thing a guy can say, and after weeks of being with me he still walks away."

I hold my hand up in the air. "That was his loss. Whoever he was. And I can't guarantee you I'll be around for forever. But I do want to see if this could be more than just a one night stand."

"You're here in New York. You do realize that right?" She looks around my apartment and says, "You may be able to last a couple of days before you'll be on the prowl again."

"You could be right. We could both realize that neither of us is capable of making this work. But what happens if we are?" As I try to prove to Nicole that this should be more than just a casual fuck I'm shocked about what I'm suggesting. I've known the girl for two days and I think I want to test the unthinkable. Most girls I meet, I fuck, then I walk away. Maybe spending all this time with her and not fucking has me disillusioned.

She's standing with her hand on her hip and her eyebrow arched. "I should get some sleep. I need to leave early in the morning."

"Shower first?" I look from my bed to her. "You know, new sheets and all." She finally cracks a smile and walks toward her bag.

"Would hate to dirty your bed." She starts the shower and leaves the door of the bathroom open. I accept that as an invitation, her agreeing to take a shower with me. I begin stripping out of my clothes from the night and join her in the shower. In the outfits she's been wearing all weekend I knew her body was bad, but seeing her completely in the nude, my dick instantly goes hard. The thought of not fucking seems absurd.

From behind her, I begin to wash her back, rubbing small circles into her muscles. She allows her head to lean forward and soft moans escape from her mouth. I continue lathering soap down her legs and when I reach her feet I turn her toward me. Her breasts are on full display, her nipples as hard as my dick.

I manage to keep my distance as the soap glides across her chest, down her stomach and above her mound. I hesitate before continuing down the front of her legs. She steps back and allows the water to wash away the suds. When the water runs clear she steps in closer to me and rubs her hand across my face and her breasts perch firmly against my chest. "What now?" She whispers.

"You can dry off. I should probably get clean too." She grabs the bottle of soap and instead of a towel she squirts the soap into her hand. Rubbing her hands together she creates a thick lather. Starting with my chest she massages soap into my skin, working down my body but avoiding my dick. I brace myself against the wall to keep my knees from buckling.

When she finishes with my body she takes her time with my dick. If I'm going to keep my word of not fucking her till her legs go weak I can't let her finish. I put my hand on hers and stop her strokes. "Let's get out of here." She looks up at me with a smirk on her face. She opens the shower door and steps out, grabbing a towel from the back of the door. I rinse off until she leaves the bathroom, and when she leaves I finish stroking my dick until I release. Grabbing a towel from the bathroom counter, I join her in my room where she's made herself comfortable between my sheets.

"These sheets are a little stiff." I can hear her legs shuffling beneath the comforter. "May need to upgrade soon."

"I'll be sure to put sheets on my house warming registry." I drop my towel and climb under the comforter with her. With my chest to her back I say, "This may be a challenge for both of us." She cradles her head into my neck and hums softly.

The sun shines brightly through the window and I jump, feeling around in the bed to wake Nicole. She has to be at the airport for her flight, and Laila and her will both kill me if she's late and misses it.

Nicole isn't in the bed. I sit up and call her name, "Nicole." The corner of the bedroom where her suitcase was last night is empty. I lay back against the pillow with my dick at full attention. I crawl out of the bed to collect my phone because my bare room lacks an alarm amongst everything else.

Six in the morning, and Nicole should be at the airport ready to board her flight. Although she snuck out like a thief in the night I decide to text her safe travels and my phone dings.

Nicole: Thanks!

This girl has me all fucked up, and my karma for fucking up women the same way is her not feeling anything for me outside of fucking. I plop onto the bed and consider ways I can get back to my old habits. The stiff sheets rub against my leg and I decide today is the day to get this damn apartment in order. Then I could have a chick here to work me over and make me forget about Nicole.

Knocking down Bryan and Laila's door, I hope Laila is available for the day to help me finish shopping for my apartment. The door swings open and Laila rolls her eyes when she sees me. "Bryan, do you know what time it is?"

I look at my phone and respond, "It's after noon. Why are you still asleep?"

She moves aside and laughs, "I had to wake up early as shit to get Nicole in a taxi." She stops and stares at me. "Why you couldn't have done that I have no idea."

Because Nicole snuck out of my apartment, probably frustrated that all we did was sleep like an old married couple. What the fuck is wrong with me? "I didn't think you would appreciate not seeing her off."

Her eyebrow arches and I'm reminded how spunky she can be. "Anyway, what did you need?" She looks back to the bedroom. "I'm dying to get my head back on that pillow."

I rock my head back and forth. "I was hoping you'd come help me finish furnishing my apartment today."

Her mouth drops and she rubs her hand over her face. "Today, Bryan?" I hunch my shoulders. "Fine." She sighs. "Let me." She pops her t-shirt. "Let me get dressed."

Chris has always been a hard sleeper. He didn't even budge as Laila got dressed and we left out of the apartment. "You like Nicole?" Laila says as she stands across from me on the elevator.

Her question catches me off guard and all I can do is laugh. Do I like Nicole? "Why do you ask?"

She swallows then looks down to her feet. "She kinda told me about last night." Of course Nicole would run and tell Laila about what happened last night. I'm definitely going back to my old ways. "Listen," she says before the elevator doors open. Two older white ladies step on the elevator and Laila goes silent.

"If you like her it's no big deal. She's a tough one, but she has to be." Laila tells me as we walk down the street to the furniture store.

"She has to be?" Nicole mentioned being left after guys sweet-talked her. I didn't put much thought into it when she said it, but maybe some dude has screwed her over. Laila looks up at me and then away before mumbling under her breath. "What's that," I ask. "I couldn't hear you."

"Nothing. It's not my story to tell."

"I'm not the commitment type either." I look down at Laila bouncing along the sidewalk. "Why change things now?"

"You can give me something better than that, Bryan. Got me out here in these streets when I could be asleep, deep in a dream right about now."

"Sounds like Nicole and I have more in common than I originally thought." Laila shrugs as we walk into the furniture store.

Instead of lagging behind me in the furniture store, like Chris, Laila is picking out furniture and accessories to complement my apartment. The store clerk and I follow behind her, and as I agree with her selections as the clerk scribbles on his notepad. "Listen Laila, it's been a minute since I've spent time with a chick, especially non-sexually. Your girl is cool as shit, and obviously sexy as a motherfucker."

The store clerk looks to me and then walks away to give us space. "And you'd want to settle down eventually, right?" I nod my head haphazardly.

She picks up a pillow then looks to me and says, "Step your game up and don't let your bruised ego get in the way."

"Easier said than done. Your girl isn't interested."

Chapter Ten
NICOLE

After swiping left on the suspect dudes popping up in the dating app I decide to login to Facebook, searching like an investigator for my old fuck buddy. Oh my God. He settled down. Scrolling through pictures of him and the same girl, I'm irritated by a few things. One, he was always my backup when I needed someone to work me over. Two, after all these years he went and found someone when he never even offered to take me on a date.

I throw my phone on the couch beside me and flip the channel to a cooking show hoping to get rid of my sexual aspirations. The chances of me getting laid tonight are just about as slim as they were last night laid up with Bryan. Still can't believe that grown ass man laid up in the bed, both of us naked, and didn't try to even rub up on me.

The Italian food on the cooking show reminds me of the little place Bryan and I went to my first night in New York. My attempt to find a dude at the bar should have been an indicator that my weekend was going to be dick-doomed. I didn't suspect, from that first night, that I would have converted Bryan into a guy who wanted to all of a sudden settle his playboy ways and be concerned about me more than sex. Why he couldn't do all that after my trip to New York is beyond me.

If I could cook, I'd run to the store for the ingredients for the Fettuccine Alfredo this chef is whipping up. He makes it seem easy, but of course he's probably had years of experience in the kitchen. My mother was too particular about her kitchen. She didn't want any of us kids in there messing up her flow. Instead she had us replace the fancy dishwasher with our hands. All these years later and I still would rather grab take-out, order delivery, or just graze on snacks before I would ever get in the kitchen.

As I'm evaluating my life and prospects of ever landing a husband, my phone dings with a message.

Laila: Ugh did you make it home?

Instead of messaging her back I call her phone. "I'm home," I say with a grin on my face.

"Heffa you should have been home hours ago. How was your flight?"

"I've been home for a while. And yes, I'm scandalous. Should have texted you when I got here. My bad."

"I forgive you." I hear someone talking in the background. "But Bryan says he was expecting a text too."

"Right. That would be boo behavior. Clearly, we aren't on that level."

Laila smacks her lips. "But you could be," she whispers in the phone.

"Laila your whispering skills are sub-par. Did you ever visit a library as a kid?" She laughs. "And what do you mean I could be?"

"Hold on," she says. I hear her moving before she continues, "I had to move away from him since you claim I suck at whispering. Anyway, I was talking to Bryan and he sounds interested in you."

"But why? I would have been the perfect fuck buddy.

Wouldn't have grown attached. Live in a completely different state. It would have been fuck buddy bliss."

"First of all what is fuck buddy bliss?" Before I can explain she cuts me off. "Never mind. Not important. Something about you has this dude messed up. I don't even think he knows why he passed up the sex. But I do know he enjoyed the time he spent with you."

"Yeah thanks to my homegirl pulling a fast one and not being available. I'm still not going to forget that by the way." I sigh. "But I'm pretty sure it all sounds good now until the next hot thing walks up to him ready and willing, and then he'll remember what a bad idea it is to be on some commitment bullshit."

"Damn, Nicole. I'm really starting to get the feeling you won't ever settle down." She may be right. I may never settle down. My first attempt at settling down was met with rejection. Being a preacher's kid, it was difficult having a boyfriend in high school. The only boy my father approved of was the deacon's son. Fortunately, he was pleasing on the eyes and wasn't as straight and narrow as everyone thought he was.

We dated, as much as high school students could date, kissed, felt each other up. Then one night, in the back of his car, he convinced me it was time to move beyond touching. We awkwardly fucked in the back seat. I thought our fates were sealed. All the dreams I had as a little girl of getting married, having a mini-me running around one day, were solidified.

Then a week later, the deacon's son decided he was over the preacher's daughter and moved on to some other church girl. I was crushed. But I vowed to myself that settling down wasn't for me. My dreams of a wedding and dreams of kids morphed into wanting to travel and have fun, alone.

"Guess I'll have to settle on being in two weddings instead of three," Laila says.

"If you are counting Jennifer into that equation you may want to check your math." She gasps. "No, her and her little boyfriend haven't broken up yet." Jennifer is the only person I have ever known who is in a relationship but noncommittal. If you leave it to her, she probably would have avoided the relationship too, but now that she's playing the role of girlfriend, that's about as far as she's going.

"Nicole, really though. I think you should give Bryan a chance."

"Listen, I'm in Georgia," I drag out Georgia for emphasis. "He's in New York. If nothing else, any shot we could have at trying a relationship is null and void for the simple fact that we can't get to know each other properly."

"You may not be able to fuck over a phone, but you can surely get to know someone." Her pleading is making me tired, and watching the food show is making me hungry. I hang up with her before I say something that could end our friendship. Being hangry can make me say crazy things.

"How was your weekend in New York?" my nosey office mate Krista asks first thing Monday morning. She turns around in her chair to face me, legs crossed with a smile on her face. We graduated the same year, but because of my extra time in undergrad, she's younger than I am. On days like today, I am reminded of that. My emails haven't completely loaded before she's digging for information.

"It was good. New York has a lot going on." I look at her and return her smile. "You should visit sometime." I remember her telling me she hadn't really ventured out of the state of Georgia where she was born, raised, and attended college. The girl is in dire need of travel time.

Krista taps her hand on her knee. "You're right. I should, so I can stop living my life through you and all my other adventurous friends." Her smile fades and I almost feel sorry for her. Almost. Although her family may not have done much traveling when she was young, she's an adult now, fully capable of booking a plane ticket and getting the fuck out of here.

"I hope we don't have a full day today. I could use the time to catch up on my document due at the end of the week." I turn to my computer and open my calendar, and I'm not surprised that it's full. "Wishful thinking I suppose." When I majored in Business Administration, I imagined walking into work wearing a power suit and making decisions that would grow an organization. Instead, I'm more like a glorified secretary attending meetings, analyzing business metrics, documenting my results, and capturing notes for those who are on the verge of retirement.

"Story of our lives," Krista sighs and turns away from me.

"What's the story of your lives?" Ethan sits on the edge of my desk and takes a sip of his coffee. The glimmer from his cufflinks mesmerizes me as I examine his suit that probably costs more than I will make in salary this week. He's where I want to be, where I thought I'd be coming out of L.U.'s illustrious business school.

Krista clears her throat and says, "You know. Just girl talk. Nothing serious." Of course she would become bashful in front of Ethan. He's a senior level manager and could have us fired, if only we reported to him. Thankfully, we don't. Ethan tugs on his beard then looks to me, shrugging his shoulders.

I grab my laptop and stand to leave our shared office space. "Excuse me," I say as I attempt to walk past Ethan. "I have to get to this meeting."

"Oh, actually I came over to ask you a question about your document." I turn to him with my eyebrows raised. "Can I walk with you?"

"Sure." I take a few steps ahead of him and he follows.

"It'll be done by the end of the week, right?" I nod my head. It would be done sooner if I weren't in meetings most of the day, but of course I don't tell him any of this. "I know it will include the quarterly marketing data." He lingers as I stand beside the conference room for my meeting. "Any way you could include the data from the social accounts?" My head swivels around. He squints his eyes. "Too much to ask?"

"I haven't reviewed the social accounts before. I'm honestly not sure if I'll be able to aggregate it by the end of the week."

Ethan bites the inside of his lip. "Okay, how about you consider it? But if you can't get it done no worries." He looks down the aisle and into the conference room. Then he whispers, "If you can make it happen, I owe you dinner."

Dinner which would be highly inappropriate considering he's a senior manager here at the company. Besides that, his skin, shades darker than mine, is smooth. Smooth like his childhood was void of puberty breakouts. His gray beard against that smooth, dark, skin makes his distinguished look too appealing to ever consider seeing him outside of this office, and definitely not in an intimate setting. Ethan smiles and says, "I mean as long as you don't have anyone who would be offended by me taking you out."

I shake my head and as the head of marketing gets closer I say, "I'll let you know what I can do." I turn away from him and take a seat at the conference table. Of course, my goal will be to add social accounts into this document, even if it means I need to lose sleep for the rest of the week. Smiling, I open my laptop and prepare myself for this meeting.

"You're amazing," Ethan smiles from across the table. Amazing and sleep deprived after pulling out all stops to make sure my document included the social accounts Ethan requested. "Order anything you'd like tonight. You deserve it." The one thing I'd love isn't on the menu.

"You didn't have to bring me out, but I appreciate it." I lay the menu on the table and say, "I've been wanting to try this place."

He squints his eyes. "Why haven't you been here yet?"

"My girlfriends are semi-cheap." I laugh. The lowest priced entree on this menu is forty dollars, and we usually dine at places where our total is more like twenty. "Anyway. I'll be sure to tell them how great it is and hopefully they'll splurge."

Ethan sighs, "Or when you're ready I'll bring you again." Without a laugh or even a smile his offer seems genuine.

"Here again? I'm sure there are other restaurants we could try." After the waitress takes our order Ethan tells me about his start at our company. Much like Krista and I, he started in documentation purgatory. After a few years, he made his way to management, and finally, to senior manager.

Our food arrives and I take a bite of my Wagyu beef and moan involuntarily. Ethan laughs and says, "Like I said, when you're ready to come here again let me know."

After my plate is void of any remnant of the beef or delicate sides, Ethan offers to buy dessert. With my nose scrunched and hand on my belly I ask, "You have room for dessert?"

The smile and glimmer in his eyes indicate what I feared. This dinner has crossed the line, and there's no turning back. I may actually get some tonight, and after the week of hustling I'm not even concerned about what our work relationship will be Monday. "My momma taught me that there's always room for dessert. Always."

"Momma's always right." Ethan orders his favorite

dessert, the New Orleans style bread pudding. After a few bites, I concede the dish to him. "I won't be able to move if I eat another bite."

"Let's go walk it off." Ethan throws his napkin on the table and calls for the waiter. After paying the bill he rises and grabs my hand. Walking is not the way I'd like to work off my full belly, but I hope it leads to more physical activity with him.

With our hands intertwined I ask, "Where are we going?"

When we exit the restaurant Ethan points down the street and says, "To the art gallery." He takes a few steps before asking, "You like art, right?" I nod my head and walk beside him. "Good." He nods his head. "This gallery features upcoming artists, and rotates the art monthly."

Ethan leads me around the gallery, pointing out distinctive details of each piece. One piece of a woman laying across a bed with a sheet draped across her body causes us both to stop and linger. Ethan whispers, "What do you think happened before the artist created this piece?"

I envision the artist and the woman from the canvas rumbling in the sheets. With my lips pursed I say, "I can only imagine."

Ethan says, "Wish I was an artist." Leaning in close to my ear he whispers, "I'd love to paint you."

"No time like the present to start practicing new ambitions." I wink at Ethan and his smile grows wide. He nods his head toward the door and I follow him, hoping we are on our way to his house to make this painting a reality. In the car, he asks me if I had enough time to walk off my food, and until then I hadn't even thought about my too full stomach. "Yeah, I'm good now." When we arrive at my apartment I'm saddened that I won't be able to see his grown man living arrangement, but it can go down in this car for all I care right now.

"Let me walk you up." He gets out of the car and opens my door. He reaches in to grab my hand and we walk up the stairs to my apartment.

When I open the door, Ethan doesn't follow me into my apartment. "Coming in?"

He wags his head. "I should probably get going. I have an early start tomorrow." Early start. On a Saturday? I scrunch my nose. "I know, sounds like an excuse." He reaches out for my hand. "But if you are free tomorrow night I'll take you up on that offer." Leaning into the door he looks around the apartment and says, "Or maybe you can come check out my place." I smile, although I feel like screaming. "I'll call you." His lips connect with mine but I pull away before I get too excited and have to fall asleep horny and pissed... again.

Closing the door, I say, "See you tomorrow." Leaning my head against the door I dig my phone out of my purse.

Nicole: You have to break this curse you have on me.

Chapter Eleven
BRYAN

As the Hennessy runs down my throat, I look around the bar at the selection of women. Most are too occupied with their friends to notice me, but there is one woman across the bar from me who is alone like myself, staring into the bottom of her now empty glass. I take the last sip of my drink then move to the seat next to her. I call the bartender over and ask, "One more Hennessy and whatever she is having."

The woman raises her hand to the bartender. "I'm good." She looks at me and whispers, "Thanks though." Her thick curls are now swept back and I have a clear view of her eyes, a greenish brown hue.

"What's your name?" I ask her as she gathers her purse in her hand.

"It's Riva." Her tongue rolling as she pronounces her name. I won't ever grow tired of the Spanish female population in New York. "Yours?"

"Bryan. Are you leaving already?" She loosens the grip on her purse.

She turns to face me completely and says, "I shouldn't

have been here for this long. I should get going or I'll regret this in the morning." I look down at my watch to check the time and it's just after nine. "I have a presentation tomorrow that I should be preparing for but instead I let my boss piss me off. Made a stop here at the bar on my way home to drink away my attitude." She rolls her eyes as I imagine she recalls the issue with her boss.

"Sorry to hear that. But I'm glad I caught you before you headed out." I place my hand over hers sitting on the bar. "Your last thoughts before you go home to prepare shouldn't be of your incident with your boss."

She takes a deep breath. "Even if you are able to rid me of my thoughts of my boss, as soon as I start to prepare for my presentation I'll be reminded of our argument." Her eyes gloss over and her irises darken. "I have to change a significant portion of the presentation." She removes her hand from beneath mine and stands to leave. "The thought alone." She shakes her head. "I should get going."

"Mind if I walk you out?" I take the last sip of my Hennessy and leave money for my tab on the bar. Following closely behind her I ask, "Do you live nearby? I could walk you home."

She cocks her head and says, "Bryan. I just met you. You could be loco." I laugh at her interjection of Spanish.

"Ah no, mami. Pero podrías estar loco." I say with a wink and she laughs with her head tilted back. She nods her head in the direction away from the bar and we walk side by side. "What type of work do you do?" I ask.

"I'm a business analyst at a financial firm." She watches her steps as we cross over a puddle of water. "On a normal day I love my job." She turns to me. "Today, not so much."

"Look at me failing on my promise. My job for this walk is to make you forget about your imperfect day." I take her hand and we continue to walk. "What about for fun?"

She stops walking and looks at the brownstone beside

us. "Maybe you can call me and I'll fill you in." She nudges her head toward her door. "Thanks for walking me home."

I pull my phone out of my pocket to collect her phone number and see a text message notification.

Nicole: *You have to break this curse you have on me.*

I dismiss the notification and input Riva's number into my phone. Although I'd rather be taking her inside, I allow her to wrap her arms around me and we hug till I feel her sigh and the tension release from her body. "I'll give you a call," I say.

On my way to my apartment I call Nicole and just before I hang up, she answers. "I have a curse on you?"

"Yup. Until I met you I could easily get some loving, a quick fix when I needed to release some stress, a rumble in the sheets just for the hell of it." I let her go on and on till her descriptions have my dick rock hard.

"Maybe we both need to find a witch doctor, because it wasn't me who cursed you. I'm having the same type of luck."

"Ain't that some shit," she says. "But maybe you deserve it for that stunt you pulled before I left New York." Nicole and I haven't spoken since she escaped my bed in the middle of the night. Not because I didn't want to, but I wanted her to reach out to me first. I told her how I was feeling, how I want more than her riding my dick on occasion. I wanted, wanted more, but now I'd settle for fucking.

"Stunt. Is that what you consider what happened," I ask. She snorts. "You still aren't convinced I'm good for more than just a good fuck?"

"I'm not even convinced you're good for a fuck." I hear her mumble under her breath. "But anyway, nothing you can do to prove either theory wrong. Or right. You're there, and I'm here."

Now she reveals her truth. She isn't down for the long

distance. "You're afraid that if I was the real deal I couldn't be true to only you." I take the stairs to my apartment to avoid losing the call in the elevator. "Because out of sight out of mind. Or some shit like that?"

"Exactly." She grunts and I imagine what she would sound like if I was delivering her pleasure. If she'd be a loud moaner or if she'd be bashful and withhold them. "You haven't had the chance to be faithful to a chick around your way, let alone one hundreds of miles away." She's right. Just as quickly as I tried to jump into the bed with Riva tonight, not seeing Nicole could be difficult.

"You're right." I take a pause to catch my breath. Since I've been in New York I've taken for granted the casual walking as an excuse to neglect the gym.

"You good? You sound like you are dying a slow and painful death over there." She laughs. "Better work up that stamina."

"I take it you're not up for a social experiment." Sometimes my mouth starts talking and shit starts rolling out without me thinking it all the way through. But I'm committed once I've said it. "A playboy and a playgirl, hundreds of miles away, stay committed to that special someone. Defying all odds." I lean against my bar and ease myself onto a barstool. Replaying what I just said, I wish I could just rewind, and go back to about thirty minutes ago before I called Nicole spewing all types of lovey-dovey bullshit.

"Damn are you coming back from the bar?" She laughs. "I'm going to chalk all that you just said to you being drunk." I'm thankful she's willing to overlook the nonsense I'm talking. But what if I was serious?

"Yeah, I should probably get off the phone before I say something that makes me lose all my street cred. If you find that witch doctor tell me what type of sacrifice I need to make to get back on track." Nicole agrees and we hang up.

Grabbing a glass from the cabinet I pour myself another Hennessy. With my drink in my hand I walk to my windows and gaze out across the city. The nightlife of New York has its beauty. The myriad of colors from the different buildings collectively makes a collage of wonder. My urge to recreate what I see is daunting me and I wish I had my art studio to escape to or at least my art supplies. My trip to Tennessee is inevitable, although I'd been avoiding going back until I figured out my next steps, but that plan makes zero sense if art is supposed to be my next step. I shake my head as I consider my void plan. Again, my mouth talking shit before my mind could think through the consequences.

My phone alerts me of a text message and I walk over to the counter and open my messages, nearly dropping my phone when I see the picture of Nicole. Not of her entirely, her face missing but her breasts on full display.

Bryan: I'm pretty sure the witch doctor didn't tell you a tits shot would break the curse

And if she did find a witch doctor who happened to tell her to send me a shot of her tits, I don't know if I owe her gratitude or attitude. My dick is sitting rock hard for the second time tonight. I'm not used to sexual deprivation.

While I wait on her to reply. I scroll through my phone and regret my no call policy. The policy that has left my phone bare of the women who have sexed me, the women who I neglect to call after our late night tryst. And then I run across Jenna's name. I pause while I debate calling her. Convincing her to let me slide through wouldn't be that difficult since she herself has requested a booty call.

But just as my thumb hovers over the call button another text comes through. This time it's a picture of her hand between her legs. I could wait to see how far she'll go, but I'm not interested in just seeing her please herself. I want to hear her. I call and she answers after a couple of rings.

"You couldn't just watch the scene unfold," she asks with a heavy voice.

"Naw. I'd much rather have the audio that accompanies these visuals." She laughs. "What were you about to send next?"

She whimpers. "I may not have sent anything else." She doesn't say another word but I can hear her breath quickening. I listen closely as I step inside my bedroom. Toeing out of my jeans I shake my head. Phone sex wasn't big back in the day, and now I'd rather the real thing, but since I can't have it, this will have to do. For now.

With my phone on speaker and my dick in my hand I lay across my bed and stroke each time I hear her moan. "Bryan you there?"

"Yeah. I'm here." I bite my lip and continue stroking.

"Late night phone sex and disappointing hand jobs." She whispers. "That's what a long distance relationship would be." I look down at my dick in my hand and consider what she's offering. "Is that really what you want for your little social experiment?"

Even with my dick in my hand I manage to disconnect from the sexual act and say, "To assure myself a relationship should be more than sex." I pause and release my dick taking the phone off speaker. "Maybe distance would be the remedy."

"Hmm," she responds as if she's taking it into consideration.

"No need to make a decision now. But before you look for another dude to sex you up think about what we could have."

"Good night, Bryan," she says before hanging up. With the phone in my hand I slide past the two pictures a few times. Then I crawl out of bed and into a cold shower to wash away the thoughts of fucking her into submission.

With the light blinding me, I shift in my bed to maintain my sleep state and my leg swipes across my dick. It has a mind of its own and is definitely cursing me for this talk of long distance loving, with no physical contact. My dreams were filled with Nicole and I guess my body was responding. I lift the covers to check out the damage. I could shoot an eye out with the build up I have. Throwing the cover back down I rummage through the bed for my phone.

Chris answers after a few rings. "Yo, Chris. I need to take…"

Before I can finish my sentence he interrupts me. "Bruh. Do you know what fucking time it is?" I move the phone from my ear to look at the time. Six in the morning. "If this isn't an emergency call me after eight."

"Damn, you're already awake now; I'll finish. I need to take a trip down to Tennessee. You up for it? This weekend probably."

"Whatever." He yawns. "I'll talk to you about it later." He hangs up the phone before I can protest.

I open my travel app and look for tickets from New York to Tennessee. With short notice, the tickets are outrageous. I find the cheapest tickets and put three of them on hold, just in case Laila wants to join us.

Before I toss my phone back on my bed I take another look at the pictures Nicole sent last night. The indiscreet photo is not only sexy but worthy of a canvas. Before I'm too tempted to paint her perky, brown nipples, I delete the pictures, erased from my phone but not my memory. I persuade myself to close my eyes and pray to the dream gods that I'll see her in la la land, perky nipples and all.

Chapter Twelve
NICOLE

Stepping over a discarded beer bottle, I roll my eyes. I spent hours getting ready for this date; my hair is laid and make-up is on point. My fitted black dress and five inch heels were chosen specifically for the purpose of convincing this dude the night needs to end in the bedroom. But here we are at an outdoor festival in the middle of downtown Atlanta. Of all the places he could have taken me, especially after seeing me dressed to impress, we are here. I shouldn't have expected too much. He did roll up on me at the grocery store with a buggy full of beer, not even craft beer, but Super Bowl Sunday advertised beer.

Sitting comfortably on the bench where he guided us to try our selection of food he says, "I should have given you a heads up on the plans for the night." He skims his eyes across my calf down to my heels. "Could have spared your heels."

Smirking I respond, "Would have been nice." I'm not beyond a pair of sneakers and a ponytail. I'm definitely not too good for outdoor festivals with sketchy food trucks, but for a first date? "Let's make the best of it now that we are here."

He smiles and my insides are excited. His button nose and perfect teeth are adorably highlighted when he smiles. His dark brown eyes and skin that blends in with the night are intriguing. It was those looks that made me look beyond his buggy full of cheap beer and give him a chance. After all, I've spent too many nights getting to know myself. The only good that has come of it has been me perfecting my act; I can finish and be fast asleep in the matter of minutes.

The thought of potentially having someone in my bed, beside me, or inside of me putting me to sleep makes me lose the attitude. Looking down at my heels I say, "They're only heels."

Kevin's hand glides down my calf and he responds, "But I must say, these heels." He stops and cups my heel in the palm of his hand. "You are definitely rocking them." He looks me in the eyes and licks his lips as if he watched LL Cool J's *Doin' It* on repeat. I raise my eyebrow to him. His hand roams back up my calf and rests on my thigh. Tracing the hem of my dress he says, "And this dress." He looks around us. "Damn, girl."

Playing with the straw of my fruit smoothie concoction I ask, "Where to next?"

"I had this speak easy spot I wanted to take you to, but…" he pauses and I'm hoping he wants to skip the bullshit as much as I do. I shift on the bench causing his hand to fall between my thighs. I smile coyly as I cross my leg over his hand. "Let's get out of here." He manages to say after stuttering over his words.

On our way to the car his hand rests casually on the small of my back, dipping ever so gently to my ass every few steps. He helps me into the car and then kneels to help me out of my heels. "I'm sure your feet may need a rest." I watch him in awe as he climbs into the car beside me. For the first time tonight, I see more in him than just a casual fuck.

"That may have been one of the sweetest things a guy has ever done," I whisper. I watch the buildings pass as we enter onto the highway in the direction of my apartment.

"You know, I think you'll enjoy the speak easy joint." He looks up the street before he makes a U-turn and enters the highway again back toward downtown.

"Have you ever performed?" His face softens and the smile he wore earlier returns. "What? Really? Feel like entertaining me till we get to the spot," I ask.

He laughs. "That's a big request. Ad-hoc poetry session while I'm driving on the highway into the city, sitting beside one of the hottest girls around." He looks my way briefly. "Not sure I can perform under all that pressure. But if you like the spot tonight, we can come back again and I may surprise you."

The idea sounds good, if there is another night after tonight. But I'm used to the broken promises, especially when it comes to dates. Most guys I've dated in the past will wine and dine you for as long as it takes to get your legs wrapped around their waist, and then morning texts turn into late night phone calls; dinner and a movie turns into chilling on my couch with take out. I look over at Kevin and mumble, "Surprise me, huh?"

We turn into a parking lot in front of a small building. From the exterior, if I had to guess, I would have bet it was a lounge by night and a cafe by day. The lights are dim inside but I can clearly make out the crowd, the crowd that is focused on the woman on stage.

"We can find a seat over there," Kevin whispers in my ear as he points to the corner opposite the entry. I navigate toward the direction he pointed to and find an empty table. As we sit the woman wraps up her poem and the crowd snaps their fingers in appreciation. "Too bad we missed the beginning. She usually has some real shit to say." I laugh at his elegant description of her poetry.

Next up is a man who takes a seat on a bar stool instead of standing like the lady before him. With the light shining in his face I strain my eyes to look at him. His resemblance to Bryan catches me off guard. When Kevin asks me a question, I have to focus before I understand what he's saying. "Yes, this place is nice."

"So we can come back again," he asks with a straight face. "Maybe a nice dinner before and you can rock another one of these dresses." He winks.

"We may be able to make that happen." I turn back toward the stage in time to hear the Bryan look-alike wrap up his piece. While the crowd shows appreciation through snaps he leaves the stage and my eyes follow him to his table. Before he takes his seat, he shakes hands with a guy, I assume his homeboy giving him props, and he kisses the cheek of a lady who is sitting with her head held high, I assume his girlfriend or wife.

On our way to my apartment I convince myself to go inside alone. My urge to sex Kevin up has disappeared. He's easy on the eyes, he has a nice body, and he could probably work me over but something deep down isn't feeling it. Something deep down is curious about what more would feel like, if maybe we could date, and I could be the girl at the table waiting for a kiss after he wraps his piece on stage. My thoughts drift to life beyond the hoe-sphere. Maybe Bryan has a point, maybe it is time for me to settle down, and stop letting these dudes get the best of me and leave me with nothing in return.

"I'll give you a call at the end of the week, and if you're free this weekend maybe we can get together." I nod my head and reach for the door before he says, "What type of man would I be if I let you climb out of the car and walk yourself to your door?" I smile and laugh to myself. He'd be like other men I've been out with in the past.

Walking to the door he grabs my hand and I confirm my thoughts from earlier. It's definitely time for a change. Farewell one night stands.

With a kiss on the cheek Kevin turns to walk away and I close and lock the door behind him. It's almost midnight, but I hope Laila is still awake.

"Hello..." she answers with a groggy voice.

"I woke you up," I say with my voice low to not fully jerk her out of her somber state.

"I mean it is, hell I don't even know what time it is." She clears her throat. "Are you okay though?"

"I am okay." I stop to think about if I'm really okay. "I'm actually great."

"Oh. What's going on?" Her voice sounds perkier like she's waking up.

"I met a nice guy and we had a really nice date tonight."

Before I can finish telling her about the date she interrupts me and says, "Aw hell. Are you really calling to tell me you broke your curse and got some tonight?"

I can hear her shuffling around. "No. The opposite."

"What?" She whispers into the phone. "Hold on I need to move to the living room before I wake Chris up." I can hear him speaking in the background. "Before I keep him up. Okay, now tell me what happened tonight?"

"I met this guy at the grocery store, and he was cute. Nice dude. He asked me to go out with him tonight."

"Wait slow down. You better not be about to tell me you met this dude and fell in love with him. Not before you've given Bryan a shot. You're supposed to be my sister-in-law," Laila says in a hurry. I'm not sure how she gathered all those pieces together considering her and Chris are not married, and Bryan and I are far from even dating, so in-law status is way off.

"Anyway. As I was saying, we went to this outdoor festival. I started off a little pissed because I was dressed for a nice dinner and we ended up there. But I got over my attitude cause I wanted to get some." Laila starts to cackle. "We were headed back to my house when he changed his mind and decided to take me to an open mic session."

"Nicole, you deserve a dude who doesn't just want to fuck." Laila can easily say that because when she met Chris she was a virgin. She teased and kept him waiting for months before she gave it up. She's never flirted with the hoe-sphere. Even when she had the opportunity to, the pressure was too much for her to handle.

"And that's what I realized tonight. I think I'm ready for more." She releases an audible gasp. "Maybe not with this dude, but in general."

"Good. There is still hope for Bryan." There is still hope for Bryan, if Bryan and I were in the same area. Although we may not be sexing it up I still would want to see him. I don't want to volunteer for a long-distance situation. After getting an update on Laila, her job, and her and Chris' shenanigans we hang up and I'm even more excited about my decision.

Chapter Thirteen
BRYAN

Nudging Chris to wake him up I say, "Bro, we are landing." He opens his eyes slightly to look at me. "You may want to wipe off the slobber that has accumulated on your chin." His eyes bulge before he realizes I'm probably bull shitting and he elbows me in the side.

"This late-night flight after a full day of work was a bad idea." Chris says while adjusting in his seat. Chris agreed to come with me to Tennessee to collect my art supplies and wrap up loose ends that I left dangling in the wind. Laila had to stay behind for a work assignment that didn't excite Chris too much, but I'm glad we'll have time to run the streets one last time.

With my luggage in tow I feel a slap on my back. "What the..."

"You had something to say," my dad looks at me with a grin. I'm both surprised to see him and surprised he's grinning, considering I quit the company and moved without much notice. We haven't had many conversations since my journey to New York.

I drop my luggage beside me and wrap my arm around

his neck. "Dad, you didn't have to pick us up. We could have gotten a taxi to my place."

"And have to track you down for five minutes of your time." I hear my mom say from behind my dad. I release my dad and wrap my mom in both of my arms. "Miss out on this moment. Yeah right. And where is your little brother?" She looks behind me.

Chris was walking slowly off the plane. I wouldn't be surprised if he is somewhere napping. Looking back toward the luggage carousel, I point him out sitting on a bench half slumped over. "He had a long day."

My mom laughs and says, "Yeah I hear his boss is a real slave driver," as she walks toward my brother. My dad clears his throat from his spot beside me. With three sons and a stubborn husband, mom has played mediator for as long as I can remember. I'm sure her side remark was an attempt to instigate a conversation between my dad and me.

Chris' approach saves us from the inevitable conversation that will come before I leave Tennessee. "Dad, you know you shouldn't have this old lady out late at night." With one arm around Mom, he shakes Dad's hand.

"From the look on your face you look like the one who shouldn't be out this late," my mom says in response to Chris. "I can't believe you didn't drag Laila along with you." Chris groans and leads us out of the airport.

My parents don't take us hostage for long; instead they drop us off at my condo with us promising to stop by in the morning. Throwing a blanket and pillow to Chris I say, "The couch should be comfortable."

"What? When we were kids we would at least sleep opposites in the bed." Chris pushes the pillows off my couch. "This couch is stiff as fuck." When he catches the smirk on my face he says, "Man, if Laila wasn't at the house I would have had you foot to head in my bed."

"We are too grown for that shit dude. You'll be straight; you only have to deal with it for a couple of nights." I sit in the chair beside the couch and say, "I mean you could sleep at the house tomorrow night." Chris rolls his eyes. "Oh, so that cheerful mood you had seeing the folks at the airport was an act?"

He hunches his shoulders. Reaching down to untie his shoes he says, "Of course I love them, but we both know you have to take everything in moderation." Except our levels of moderation are totally different; I'm on a chat for a few minutes' vibe and his is more like have lunch or dinner. "Throw me a towel." Chris stands up and walks toward the bathroom. "I need to wash off the funk from the airplane."

Passing by my gallery wall in the hall I grab towels for Chris and yell through the door, "Open up, here you go." Taking more time to look at my art I'm inspired, again, by some of the pieces. Over the years I've gathered a variety of pieces in my hall. Pieces that could easily be sold to an art enthusiast but that have significant meaning, and I keep them close by. But my favorite, a sunrise over Lookout Mountain, is the centerpiece. Because I don't plan on getting rid of my condo anytime soon, I leave the pieces on the wall. From my studio, I start packing my art supplies, mostly my paint brushes and collection of paint. An unfinished canvas ordains my easel, a piece I started before I left. Sitting down in front of the easel, I dip my brush in brown paint and my hand begins stroking across the canvas.

The curves flow naturally, but the hues of the blue took me a while to perfect. "Is that who I think it is?" Chris asks from behind me. His yawn causes me to turn around.

"You should go to sleep. Why are you still awake?" I ask him.

He squints his eyebrows then points to the window.

"Man, I've been sleep. Obviously you haven't." I turn to look at the sun shining through the window. "Have you been up all night working on this?"

Focusing on the painting I realize I have been at it for a while. I took the canvas that had a few elements on it and now it's completely painted. Obviously it's far from complete, but it's been a while since I've painted, and I lost track of time. "Guess I have been up all night. You know how I get when I'm in my groove."

Chris walks around the room admiring other pieces. "No, you started all this while I was in college. Mom bragged about some of your pieces, and I've seen a few but never realized how deep your passion ran." He stands behind me and asks again, "And this one?"

"Even more than my creativity, I amaze myself with my memory." I look at the detail of the dress. "She wore this dress the day before she left New York."

"Still can't win her over?" I shake my head. "She called Laila the other night. Something about being ready to settle down."

"What? She found someone?" He hunches his shoulders and walks toward the door.

"I don't know if she found someone but maybe if you try a little harder she'll be ready for you." Try a little harder? Says the guy who didn't have to do much for his live-in girl-friend to fall madly in love with him. If I remember Laila's recollection correctly, his approach to her was a major turn-off but she was already attracted to him. Lucky bastard.

"Too bad you can't give me any advice," I say walking behind him to the kitchen. "I don't even know what I'm saying. Do I really want to be with the same woman for any stretch of time?"

"You're right. I can't give you any advice." He starts a pot of coffee. "I've never been a playboy trying to get a playgirl." He opens and shuts most of my cabinets before realizing there isn't any food. "Bryan, the cabinets are empty. Did you ever grocery shop?"

I shake my head. "For the most part I ate out. Or crashed Mom's for dinner." He leans against the counter looking defeated. I feel the night weighing on me. "I'm going to get a few hours of sleep in, and then we can go to Mom and Dad's before hitting the streets." I smile at the idea of us roaming the streets together. Before I left for college, Chris was too young to hang with me, and when I came back, our parent's didn't want me to corrupt him his last years of high school.

"We should probably pick up David too." I smirk. "I know he probably won't be up for hanging with us." David, a few years older than me, acts more like an uncle than an older brother at times.

Walking to my room I say, "Wake me in a few hours."

Just as I get comfortable, naked across my bed with the sheet covering my waist, my phone goes off, a message notification that I contemplate ignoring until the second notification alerts me.

Mrs. Davenport: I hear you are in town.

I thought my Mom was done communicating with Mrs. Davenport; at least I would have assumed she would have been done talking to her after our shit hit the fan.

Bryan: Just for the weekend. Grabbing my art supplies.

I turn the sound of my phone off and roll over. Nothing Mrs. Davenport could say right now is enough to keep me awake.

By the second blow to my head I swing my arm in the air aiming to hit whoever is in arm's reach. "What the fuck," Chris says. "You still sleep naked." He throws a blanket over me. "Get up, you've been sleep long enough. Mom's been blowing me up."

Chris is dressed and standing above me. "Okay. Okay.

I'm up." Chris doesn't budge. "Unless you want to see how God had no more to bless you with after me you should move."

Chris laughs and throws another pillow at me then walks out the door. While the water heats up in the shower I look over the messages from Mrs. Davenport. Even after all she risked the first time around, she still wants to see me. Mr. Davenport happens to conveniently be out of town too. Shit, who am I to neglect her?

Bryan: I'll meet you there at ten.

"Like out in public?" Chris asks. I nod my head as I drive down the street to our parent's house. "Yeah that's probably the worst idea you ever had." He claps his hands together. "Actually, the second worst idea. The first being your random move to New York."

"All the other old people of the city should be sleep around then anyway. And Mr. Davenport is out of town." I park in the driveway and say, "Let's make this quick." I look over at David's car. "See if your punk ass brother will leave with us."

My mom greets us at the door with her arms wide open ready to receive us, as always. "Is that what grown people do in New York?" Chris and I exchange a look before she continues, "Sleep in all day." She ushers us into the door. "I had breakfast ready for you both, but I could only hold off your dad and David for so long before they devoured it."

"Aw Ma, you didn't have to do all that," I say, wrapping my arm around her shoulders.

She looks over her shoulder at Chris walking behind us. "Who are you kidding, honey, I know you have no food at that house. Starving my baby. I know he has to be hungry."

"You got that right, Ma," Chris says as he bombards the kitchen.

Before my dad appears I ask my mom, "Why'd you tell

Mrs. Davenport I was in town?" She looks up at me with her mouth agape.

"Bryan, I was at the grocery store picking up food for you boys. I ran into her on my way out and let my excitement get the best of me." She rolls her eyes. "I didn't think she was bold enough to say anything to you."

"It's cool, Ma." Of course I won't tell her the plans I have for Mrs. Davenport tonight. I'll keep those details to myself. "What else did you grab from the store?" I ask wriggling my brows.

"Should have been here for that breakfast." David rises from the bar stool to embrace me. "Ma went all out... we had biscuits and gravy, bacon, omelets, fresh fruit, fresh squeezed orange juice."

Chris shuts the refrigerator and says, "And y'all ate it all?" He leans against the counter with a glass of orange juice. "I'm going to need to get some food quick or I'm going to be one angry..." He stops mid-sentence to make eye contact with Mom.

Mom looks Chris square in the eye and says, "Little boy. I'm done for the day. You better ask one of your brothers to take you out for lunch." She makes her round of hugs before exiting the kitchen.

I look at David and Chris and say, "Let's get out of here."

David puts his hand up interrupting me. He says, "Out before you even speak to Dad." He snickers. "We'll be hearing about that for too long. At least stop by his office before we leave out."

Chris nods in agreement. "Yeah we have to give Pops some love or we'll never hear the end of it."

We find our dad signing papers in his office. I tap on the door and he looks up with a smile on his face. Waving us in he says, "Come on in boys." He looks at each of us and says, "It's been a while since I've had all three of you together."

He puts his pen down and leans back in his chair. His eyes are weary and his hair is grayer than before I left Tennessee. After all these years, his age is catching up to him. "I didn't realize how much I miss the full house." *My dad being emotional?*

Growing up my mom was the natural nurturer. Our dad was always the hard worker, making sure we had everything we needed and lecturing us on the things we wanted before giving in and buying them for us. We rarely saw him excited about our accomplishments, but he made sure we knew when we disappointed him. Thankfully, my mom swooped in after he expressed his thoughts.

"Where are y'all headed?" my dad asks.

"I need some food in my stomach. Bryan had nothing, not even a cracker in his house." Chris looks at me with his eyebrow raised. "Then he had the nerve to sleep too long and make me miss Mom's breakfast." Chris turns to look at my dad, who is laughing.

"That sounds about right. When Bryan was here he stayed in the kitchen rummaging for anything your mother cooked." My dad rubs his stomach. "But sorry y'all had to miss out on breakfast; your mother showed out as usual."

Chris stands up and says, "All this talk of food is just making things worse." He walks behind Dad's desk, giving him a hug. Dad stands from his seat and moves to the front of the desk leaning against it. David hugs him next and they both walk out of the office.

I stand next, ready to give my dad a hug, but he stops me. "Give me just a minute, Bryan." His voice is a bit sterner than it had been a few minutes ago. I'm ready for him to tell me about how I've let him down in life. My shoulders hunch over and I sit back down. "We didn't have a chance to talk about your departure from the company. I can't tell you how surprised I was to hear that you were leaving. And suddenly."

"Dad, I needed to get out of here and if I thought about it for too long I wouldn't make any moves."

Nodding his head he says, "I understand. You've always gone against the grain." He smiles widely and the tension that had started building in my shoulders is released. "Something they say about middle children." My dad being a middle child should know all about the characteristics we share. "You know you can always come back. But I hope you are successful with your art." He looks around his office then back to me. "Maybe you can find time to create a piece for the office."

I nod my head and smile. Standing I pull him into a hug, and I know he's finally come around to accept my decision to leave the company. "We'll stop by before we leave tomorrow."

He pats my back and says, "You better."

David and Chris are leaning against my car. "Time for some food," I say to Chris as I climb into the driver's seat. David climbs into the passenger seat beside me. "David you hanging tonight?"

The smirk on his face gives me all the answer I need but I egg him on anyway. "What's the rush to get home, old man?" He looks at me with a smirk on his face. "We are only in town for one more night. You need to kick it with us." I look in the rearview mirror at Chris and continue, "Besides next time you see your brother he may be on serious lock down."

David says, "What?" Turning around to face Chris he asks, "You ready to get married?"

"You know your brother. Always running his mouth. He may beat me down the aisle." David turns to me with his mouth wide open.

"You mean Mr. Don Juan himself? Settling down? I won't ever believe that myth," David says, followed by a gut-wrenching laugh.

"Good don't. It's as fake as Santa Claus and the Tooth Fairy." I put the car in park at Tupelo Honey and say, "But he's being modest about his relationship with Laila. I won't be surprised if we aren't groomsmen by next year." I slap David's gut and say, "Make sure you get that under control. Don't want to look a mess in your tux." Chris laughs as he gets out of the car.

The basket of biscuits that the waitress delivers to our table is practically gone before she takes our food order. David catches us up with the behind the scenes action happening at the company. When I was in the office there was always a fair share of drama. The ladies who varied in age kept a mouthful of gossip about one another.

David, favoring my dad more as he ages, shifts in his seat. "One of the gossiping ladies told me that Mr. Davenport is looking to sell their Tennessee properties again." I look up from my Bloody Mary and listen as he continues. "They think he's about to liquidate his assets before divorcing the missus. Of course all speculation." He eyes me and waits for my response.

"Better be careful meeting that woman tonight." Chris looks at me then laughs. "I'd hate for Mr. Davenport to be trailing her to prove her indiscretions so he can avoid paying her in the divorce."

David coughs then says, "You're meeting up with her tonight?" He, like my dad, was beyond pissed about the affair and all the negative attention it brought to our firm. "Dad just got over everything that happened."

"Man, I don't plan on doing anything with that woman," I say to David before looking over at Chris with the big mouth. "And if someone follows us they won't have any proof of what we'll be doing." Our food arrives to the table and thankfully they are both too captivated with eating to say anything further about my meeting tonight.

On our way out of the restaurant we bump into one of

the gossiping ladies from the firm. "Bryan, Chris. Good to see you both. I heard you all were going to be here this weekend." She eyes both of us then says, "Looking good." Looking at David she leans in and gives him a lingering hug.

Outside we question David about the chick. David has always been one to keep his love life close to his heart. As far as we know he isn't in a relationship, but like me, he could be messing around with a few girls. "It's nothing," he says, keeping his response too short to be believable, but we let him have it.

My phone rings after dropping off David at my parent's house. "Bryan." I recognize her voice although I haven't heard it in a while, even through what sounds like whimpering. "Can we meet earlier?" she asks.

I look over at Chris before pulling out of the driveway. With my hand over the mouthpiece I ask him, "Mind if I flake on our plans?"

He yawns and shakes his head. Grabbing the handle of the door he says, "I'll stick around here. Pick me up later." With his hand still on the door he looks at me and says, "Don't do anything to get yourself caught up."

"Same place," I ask her. She confirms and I head in the direction of the bar. My original plan to stay out of sight of anyone who would recognize her is diminished by meeting her this early.

Inside the bar there are people sitting at the surrounding tables and only a few at the bar. I find a seat away from the others and wait for Mrs. Davenport to arrive. While I'm waiting, I notice one of the older ladies I painted a picture for sitting across from me at the bar, one of Mrs. Davenport's close friends. She appears to be closing out her check and preparing to leave. To avoid awkward contact I keep my eyes on my drink until I hear her walk out.

"Bryan, thank you for coming earlier," I hear Mrs. Davenport say from behind me. "Mind if we get a table?" I turn around to face her, noticing her always perfect face is distressed. Her make-up is smeared and her hair looks like she was caught in a storm on her way into the bar.

"Are you okay," I ask as I pull out her chair at the table. "What's going on?" Concerned I look over my shoulder to check the surrounding tables for anyone who may have noticed her come in and sit with me.

"It's Alonzo." Her husband's name makes me cringe. I've never been on a first name basis with him, and after our affair I definitely kept his name far from my thoughts. "I think he's leaving me."

"Where is all of this coming from? What happened?" I lean forward in my seat and place my hand near hers. She slides her hand off the table raking it through her hair.

"I found out that he was selling the properties here in Tennessee." She looks to me and I raise my brows to fake concern, although this isn't news to me. "When I confronted him about it tonight he told me it was time for us to go our separate ways and he had no plans of remaining here in Tennessee." The man is ruthless, especially considering her infidelity was to spite him because of his.

"Mrs..." I stop and correct myself; she's never cared for me being formal with her. "Veronica, you have a lot going on. Do you think it's a good idea for us to be out?" I look at her to gauge her reaction. "Together?"

Her head swings back and she laughs. "Really, Bryan, what more do I have to lose?" With wealth, comes power, and Mr. Davenport has plenty of money. Her lifestyle as she knows it could be over. "Have time for a drink?" She smiles. "Or two?"

I nod my head and we order drinks and I fill her in on my life in New York. She's most interested in the art I've done since I've been there and is disappointed to hear that it's been minimal. After our second drink she asks, "Follow me to the hotel?" I hesitate until her finger rubs circles into the back of my hand. My body reacts before my mouth can verbalize a response.

When I agree I tell her to go ahead of me while I close out the tab. She puts a room key in my hand and whispers, "Room 405," then stands and walks out of the bar.

On my drive to the hotel I contemplate what's about to happen next. Mrs. Davenport is passionate in the sheets; for her age she's more flexible than most girls I've dealt with half her age. But the aftermath may not be worth the reward. My dad will probably digress, my mom will certainly be disappointed, and Mr. Davenport who knows what will happen if he finds out about us this time around.

She opens the door dressed in a sheer black robe. Her hair has been combed, her make-up has been removed, and she looks better than she did at the bar. She pulls me into the room by my hand. Once I'm inside she releases it and grabs my face, pulling it into hers, kissing me with her body flush against mine.

Of course my body responds, and my hands begin to roam her body, exploring her bare breasts, taking my time with each of them before leading a trail to her stomach and finally between her legs. She moans in response, her body moving closer to mine. We inch closer to the bed as our kiss deepens. When she lays across the bed, and her robe falls open to expose her nakedness, I pause.

"Bryan, baby, what's wrong?" All the potential responses to that question rush my thoughts at once and I just shake my head. "I thought you wanted this is as much as I did."

Instead of shaking my head this time I say, "I did." Closing my eyes and taking a deep breath I continue. "I just can't."

"Don't worry about Alonzo. I told you, we're done. Won't have to worry about his backlash. Ever." Although that should concern me, it doesn't and my eyes narrow as she stares at me.

"Oh Bryan, is it someone else?" She closes her robe and pats the bed beside her. "I didn't recognize it until now. Before you were living wild and free, but you found someone in New York, didn't you?"

Sitting beside her I say, "It's not that at all. I just need to get my shit together and rocking the boat with my family again isn't something I need right now." I look at the door and stand again. "I should get going. We have an early flight in the morning." She follows me to the door and I give her a hug before I open it. "Take care, Mrs. Davenport."

She kisses my cheek and says, "I hope it all works out for you, Bryan." With my head hanging low I leave the room, not turning back, not allowing myself to get tangled in the web of issues that will follow if I allow my body to control me.

Chapter Fourteen
NICOLE

"Who is it?" I hate unexpected visitors. Nobody responds but the knocks get louder. I'm tempted to leave them on the doorstep for showing up and knocking on my door like the damn police. "I'm coming, shit." I check the peephole before opening the door. What? I pull the door open and say, "Bryan? What? How?"

He smiles and wraps me in his arms. Behind him I see a few bags and I step back. "Planning on staying a while?" I laugh as I remember Laila describing how he showed up on their doorstep unannounced with his bags.

He laughs and shakes his head. "Not unless you want me to." He kisses my cheek and asks, "Can I come in?"

I move out of the way then realize I never left the house today. I've been lounging around in sweats all day with a bare face. Shit. I put my hand to my head and feel my hair wrap still in place. What a perfect time for Bryan to show up. I'm looking a hot ass mess. I look over at him and he looks well put together.

He sets his bags down near the couch and I ask, "How did you know where I live?" He smirks and slants his head.

"Oh, right." Laila would give him my details and keep me in the dark. She's determined to get us together.

I sit on the couch and he sits beside me. With his hand on my head he says, "You look comfortable." Considering it's too late to hide, I shrug. "You still look good though." He pats my leg. "I like this look on you." He puts his arm around my shoulder and pulls me into him. "Did you have any plans for today?"

Considering it's Sunday and I attended Bedside Baptist and binged Netflix all day I think I'm all in for the day. But I don't want to sound like a total bum. "I was about to get ready to pick up some food."

"Great, mind if I come with you?" He's speaking like he has no plans of leaving anytime soon and still hasn't explained why he's here.

"Sure. Give me a few minutes to get dressed." I hand him the remote and say, "Make yourself comfortable."

In my bedroom I close the door behind me and grab my phone. I escape to the bathroom to avoid being heard. "Laila, what the hell?"

Laila laughs on the other end of the phone. "He actually came over?"

"Actually came over? Why didn't you warn me? I'm wearing sweats and my hair is wrapped." Looking in the mirror I pat my bare face. "Not a lick of make-up on my face. What is he doing here?"

She sighs and says, "He just called and asked for your address. Fortunately, I still had it from when I sent your birthday gift a few months ago." She rambles on about being happy he called her for it, but she avoids my main question.

"Laila. Answer the question girl."

"Oh." She goes silent. "I guess he never told me what he was coming for. Do you hate me?"

"No, I don't hate you. Glad I wasn't in here laid up with

Kevin. Or anyone. Next time Laila, give me a heads up." She apologizes and I rush off the phone considering I need to come up with dinner plans all of a sudden.

"Ready?" Bryan looks up from the couch and we make eye contact. His mouth curves into a sexy smile and my stomach does a flip.

He stands and says, "I love when a girl can look as beautiful in comfortable clothes as she can all dolled up." Placing his hand under my chin he moves toward my mouth and kisses me, short and sweet; when the kiss doesn't linger I'm disappointed. "What'd you plan on eating tonight?"

Smiling wide I tell him, "There's this place in mid-town I like." Walking toward the door with him following behind me, my Sunday is ending much better than it started.

Surprisingly there is no wait at Front Page News, and we are seated away from the band. I have a million questions for Bryan, and I'm happy I won't be screaming over the music or straining my ears to hear his responses.

"I know you're wondering what I'm doing here in Atlanta," Bryan says as he's sitting comfortably in his seat. "I should have been on a flight back to New York with Chris, but this morning I had this strong urge to see you."

My eyebrows raise as he confesses he wanted to see me. Bryan has never been shy about telling me how he feels, so there is no surprise there, but I honestly thought that was for the weekend while we were in New York. A ploy to seduce me. "Tell me more about this urge you had."

He laughs. "I told you. I'm still interested in getting to know you. And I know you have an issue about the distance."

"Being spontaneous must be nice." I look around us then back to him. "Maybe I need to find a career in art." He laughs then leans forward. "How'd your trip to Tennessee go anyway?" Having spent the majority of his life in Tennessee, I'm sure he has a long list of females he can call that would be ready and willing.

"It met the purpose." He sighs. "It did remind me that I miss having space in my place to paint. That'll be the hardest adjustment in New York." I nod my head in agreement. I couldn't live in New York unless I had the money to stay in a penthouse with multiple rooms and lots of space. A few more days in Laila's apartment would have had me going crazy.

"Where will you paint when you get back?" I'm assuming that he is going back to New York and doesn't plan to move in with me on a whim.

"I'm looking for a studio, hopefully, one that is nearby because when I start painting I get caught up and have long nights." I wish I had something I was passionate enough about to stay up for hours and lose track of time. I definitely couldn't get that caught up in the work I do. Every hour in the office I'm counting down my time. Hell I count down the minutes; watching the clock is a constant exercise for me. "My first night back in my place I stayed up all night working on a piece." He looks at me with a crooked smile.

"What's that smile about?" I ask.

"Just thinking about the piece I was working on." He adjusts in his seat. "I'd like to show you my work one day."

I tell him about my trip to the art studio and told him I was surprised to be interested in the art. I think that has more to do with him and less to do with the art. I'm intrigued by his world, about the passion that inspired him to walk away from his cushy life of privilege and guaranteed income.

"Next time I visit we can check it out again." My eyebrows scrunch together. He laughs and says, "I plan to visit often; maybe it'll help you get over the distance." I cough but the words I try to speak are stuck in my throat. "Tell me who you went to the art exhibit with." His eyebrow raises and his smile spreads. Most of my dates ended in no loving and I would promptly call Bryan to complain. He's aware that my sex life has been absent since my trip to New York.

"It was a guy from work." Bryan leans in to hear more. Taking a bite of our appetizers he stares ahead at me. "Nice dinner, art exhibit, and then he dropped me off with a kiss on the cheek." I laugh. "With these plans to visit me, I hope you plan to end this curse we are both under." After saying those last words I look down at the table. I hadn't considered, although he spoke of having no luck with the ladies, this weekend he could have been laid up with one of his old flings. "At least the curse that has its hold on me."

"I'm starting to believe it isn't a curse at all." Bryan reaches for my hand and rubs his finger across my knuckles. "Maybe it's the universe preparing us for more." With my opposite hand, I rub the back of my neck. After a few weeks of little contact, his simple gesture has my sex peaked. "I'm thinking I'll stay around for a couple of days and spoil you before going back to New York."

"Do you consider New York home?" Bryan shifts in his seat and looks down before looking back at me. "Both times you've mentioned New York you haven't called it home yet."

"Oddly enough, I don't consider it home yet." He laughs. "That could be because I crashed on Chris' couch for the first few weeks. That felt like a horrible vacation." He looks away then back to me. "Maybe once I have an art studio set up it'll feel more like home."

"What are your plans while you're here?" Our waiter returns to the table with our entrees. We both pause at the sight of the food in front of us and thank the waiter.

"Obviously I know you have to go to work. Unfortunately." Unfortunately is correct. If I could replay our New York weekend skipping work and instead playing with Bryan, my week would be made. But my bills would be unpaid.

"Until I find a craft that I can monetize, I'll have my ass at work."

"While that cute ass is at work I'll explore the city. Find some places for us to check out together." After chewing my bite of food, I smile. He's taking this 'get to know you' phase seriously. I'm impressed.

"Then it'll be back to reality for me. I need to get some pieces on the market before I'll need to return this ass to a daytime job." We finish our food and Bryan says, "I saw something that looked pretty good on that dessert menu." Licking his lips, he continues. "But to be honest what's across the table from me looks about ten times better than anything they can bring from that kitchen."

With my eyebrow arched I say, "Let's get out of here then." Bryan nods his head and asks the waiter for the tab.

While walking to the car, Bryan's hand rests on my ass. The thought of Kevin pops into my head, from our evening at the festival. It was with him when I realized I wanted to stop having random sex encounters. But here I am hoping Bryan devours me as soon as we step into my apartment. I want him to work me over enough to have me walking like I finished a session of SoulCycle.

I thrust the door of the apartment open and throw my purse on the counter. Turning to Bryan I wait for him to dig into his dessert. "Need a drink?" I ask walking toward the refrigerator. With the refrigerator door open, I reach for a bottle of water to cool me down. My body is feeling warmer than the sun outside. Then I feel his lips on the back of my neck and his arm snaked around my waist.

"You're warm, you feeling okay?" He asks. I close the refrigerator and nod. Turning me around we lean against the kitchen counter. He reaches into the freezer, grabbing a cube of ice. "Let's see if this will help." Rubbing the ice down my neck, he licks the trail of water that is left behind. Instead of cooling down I feel warmer, warmer in all the right places. I place a hand on each side of his waist and with my eyes closed, I let my body react to each sensation.

With the ice fully melted and each trace removed from my neck, Bryan moves his mouth to mine. With a kiss lasting longer than the one earlier, I begin to moan. My hands make their way around his neck and hold him closer. Our kiss ends and Bryan leans his head against mine. "As much as I want to see how long I can last without sexing you, I don't think I can hold out too much longer." He leans against the counter beside me.

Reaching out for his hand I say, "I think we've both lasted as long as we can." I tug him toward me and lead him to my bedroom. Removing my clothes, I lay on the bed while he kicks out of his shoes. I watch patiently as he pulls his shirt over his head and toes out of his pants.

He looks at me with his body on full display. A body that, at his age, could compete with some of the younger guys I've been with. His abs are not ripped, but defined, and his biceps are not bulging, but visible. With a mischievous smile he says, "You sure about this?"

I couldn't be more sure about this. It's been months since I've had intimacy beyond a few short kisses. It's the longest period I've gone with no sex, a long, lonely, period that I hope not to repeat anytime soon. "More than you'll know." As he climbs into the bed beside me I realize that I could go through another dry spell because he isn't just down the street. I won't be able to call him over for a late night rendezvous or creep into his bed in the middle of the night. But I'll worry about those details later.

With his body closer than we've been I feel his bulge

against my leg and his hand on my face as he brings me in for a kiss. My leg gravitates across his and I fight my urge to climb on top of him. Not wanting our time to end too soon, I avoid my desires to mount him and ride him until I reach my peak. His hand caresses my chest and he moves his mouth toward my neck.

My hands roam his body, exploring his abs and lingering around his waistline just above his boxers. Although his chest is bare, I can feel hair protruding from his boxers. As his mouth covers my breast my hand dips into his boxers and I'm not disappointed; my arousal is uncontrollable. Between moans I ask, "Do you have a condom?" Without moving his mouth from my chest his hand drops from the bed and he hands me a condom. I take that as my cue to get to work.

Rolling on top of him, and lowering his boxers I position the condom and myself. We make eye contact before I start to rock my hips. I break our eye contact and my head drops back as I feel myself losing control. Bryan grabs my head and pulls me into him for a kiss. With his tongue deep inside of my mouth and his dick deep inside of me, my thighs begin to quiver. Bryan grabs me and rolls me off of him. "Not yet," he whispers before slipping back inside of me. Over my dry spell I've gotten to know myself, and getting to the point quickly was always the goal. Now my body is betraying me. My stamina can't keep up with his even as he slows down his movements.

Our eyes connect again and Bryan smiles, "Guess it's been too long," he says. I nod and smile back. "We have time to make up for it." And he thrusts, sending me into ecstasy. With my hands gripping his hips he continues until my body stills. With a kiss to my forehead he lays beside me. "You good?"

With a sigh I say, "Better than good." I raise my head and despite the sleepiness trying to keep me still I crawl out of the bed and look back at Bryan. "Join me for a shower?" After a day like today I could use a warm shower and cleaning myself by myself would be wise but departing from Bryan feels uncomfortable.

Bryan shrugs and says, "You don't ever have to worry about me turning down an invite from you."

Chapter Fifteen

BRYAN

"I'll meet you back in New York in a few days." I didn't explain my next steps to my brother and he hesitated before parting ways with me at the airport. But by the smile he gave me before he was out of sight, I knew he understood.

Not going to New York was what felt right, and being with Nicole was definitely what I needed, especially after my encounter with Mrs. Davenport. Now opening and closing Nicole's cabinets in search for a pan, I'm certain I made the right choice coming to Atlanta.

Eggs, bacon, and bread are on deck for a decent breakfast. Considering Nicole only had a can of instant coffee in her kitchen, I hope she'll be happy for the change in her morning routine. I eased out of bed after she left me for the bathroom and had to squash my goal of cooking half-naked in her kitchen when I had to get dressed to run to the grocery store.

"Let me find out on top of everything else you can cook." Nicole sits at her table with her purse perched beside her. "Taking me to dinner, putting me to bed." She said that with a crooked smile. "Sending me to work with a full stomach." She sits back in her seat. "Be careful, I may not let you leave." She winks at me. If she only knew how much I wouldn't object to her asking me to stay. Most women don't have the luxury of staying with me overnight, and I would never wake up early to make them a meal. Hell, most women don't even get a second call from me.

"The least I could do for you letting me crash your Sunday." I still haven't decided how long I'm staying and certainly don't want to overstay my welcome. "What time do you usually get off?" I'll tour the city while she's at work and return in time to be here when she gets home. "Wait." I stop flipping the eggs and say, "Damn. I didn't consider the fact that you could have plans today or this week." I look at her cautiously, hoping she doesn't give me the boot.

She pulls out her phone and scrolls through it. "My calendar is free for the..." she looks up to me with her head leaning to the side, "week."

Laughing I continue flipping the bacon before throwing a plate together for her. "Eat up before you're late for work."

She obeys, taking a bite of the bacon. "How'd you know I would partake in the swine?"

"Did you forget you ordered bacon wrapped shrimp for dinner last night?" I ask with my eyebrows cocked. Taking a seat beside her I say, "What time do you need to be at work?"

She shrugs and closes her eyes. I assume she has the same feeling about work as I did when I had to go into an office every day. After years of the same routine I am enjoying making my own schedule, waking naturally instead of from an alarm clock, staying up late to paint and not worrying about having zero energy to be productive the next day. "I should get going soon. I have a daily nine o'clock meeting."

"Do you work close by?"

"About twenty minutes with traffic." She pushes her eggs around her plate. After only a small bite I assume she isn't a fan, and take note for the next time I decide to be domestic. Looking at her watch she says, "Thank you for cooking. Don't know the last time I had a home-cooked breakfast."

Living close to my mom as an adult had its advantages. Breakfast, lunch, and dinner were readily available. I just had to drop in, and I'd be guaranteed a hot meal, no matter the day of the week. Nicole stands, taking our plates to the kitchen. "Hey Nicole, let me know if I'm invading your space or if you're ready for me to leave."

Nicole throws her hands in the air. "You don't have to worry about me kicking you out." She grabs her purse from its spot on the table and lingers near me. She looks at me while she fondles her purse handles.

I stand and pull her by the waist into my chest. With my mouth on her lips before she can pull away, I give her a short but passionate kiss, just enough to keep me on her mind all day. Pulling away I slap her on the ass and say, "Better get to work." I look down at her when she doesn't move and laugh. "I know it's tough. I could definitely take you back to bed with me right now and put us both back to sleep."

With that she turns and walks toward the door. "With words like that you'll have me losing my job." She waves and walks out of the door. I return to the kitchen to clean my mess and hear the door re-open. "The spare is in the top drawer over there," Nicole points, "If you leave you'll be able to get back in. See you later."

My plans for Atlanta were to stop in and seduce Nicole and be on my way. But after seeing her, especially after feeling her, I think my stay extended itself. Like Friday night when I painted for hours and lost track of time, with Nicole as my muse, I have an urge to paint. I sent my gear back with Chris, so I'm hopeless, but the urge is nagging me.

When I return to the bedroom to retrieve my phone I see my luggage neatly near Nicole's closet. The bed has been made and the room looks as if what happened last night, never happened. Instead of climbing back in the bed and reclaiming some of my lost sleep, I retrieve my phone and head for the couch.

Searching for an art studio to squat in for the day is unsuccessful. If I wanted to take Nicole out for a date there are plenty of the paint and sip variety, but that would do nothing for my creativity. I could just grab a paint by numbers workbook from the store. In the middle of my search, my phone rings.

"Hello," I say waiting for Chris to ask me a million questions that deserve no response.

"How was it," he asks.

"Nicole is good. I'm glad I came here instead of going back. Did you drop my stuff off in my apartment?"

"If you're still there I assume she didn't kick your intruding ass out," his tone condescending. Like Nicole would want to kick me out. I'm growing on her, slowly tearing down that wall she's built up over the years.

"Why would she kick me out?"

Chris laughs and in the background, I can hear what sounds like the office manager asking him a question. "We'll get into that another time. Maybe when you are back." He responds to the office manager then asks, "When are you coming back?"

"I haven't decided yet." I don't want to monopolize too much of Nicole's time. When I plan a trip to visit, instead of this surprise visit, I'll stay for longer. "I'll be home this week though. Miss me already?"

"Not at all, but I must admit I am jealous. Not having a schedule to live by, doing what the hell you want. And. And having Dad's approval. Must be nice." I scoff at his remark regarding Dad's approval. Obviously, I'm not his favorite kid. "When you get back let me know if you need a ride from the airport." We hang up and I start looking for a flight.

After I have a flight booked, a fresh shower, and Nicole's key in my pocket I leave her apartment. On my way to an art studio I finally found, I call to check on Nicole. When she answers I ask, "What was the name of that art exhibit you visited?"

"Hey there mister." The sound of her voice causes me to shift in my seat. I'm sure she doesn't intend to sound like a phone sex operator but if she needed a part-time job she's in there.

"Are you busy?" I should have led with that question.

"Not entirely, and the name of the place is Soulful Expressions." I saw that place in my search results.

"Thanks. Get back to work. I'll see you in a few hours." Before she hangs up I hear someone in the background giggle.

I've heard driving around Atlanta can be a nightmare. But during this time of day, not many cars are on the road. But even if traffic was at a full stop I'd enjoy being in the car. When I go back to New York I'll be shuffling around on foot or in the back of a taxi. I take my exit for the art studio and I'm pleased to see the graffiti that adorns the building and surrounding parking area. Walking in I pass a few eccentric types and I feel at home.

My spot in the studio is quiet, but I can hear music blasting from a room nearby. Everyone creates in their own element and once I get into the flow the only thing that matters is the paint and the canvas. Fortunately, the studio has art supplies on deck. I set up my canvas and grab the colors that have been coming to mind all morning.

With my first strokes, the canvas changes from the stark white to a soft yellow.

As I build the painting, I choose a smoke gray for her sweat pants, and rose red for her shirt. But when I begin painting her head wrap I use a mixture of colors. As it comes together I laugh because I realize that although she was comfortable, and probably took little effort in throwing her outfit on that morning, it all came together. Even in her mess, she's still perfect.

I'm satisfied with the smile that I was able to capture. Certainly, it's her best attribute. I add in a few background details and place my paintbrush on the table beside the easel. I stand, taking a few steps back to gaze at the final piece. I came here to release my creative juices but after viewing this piece I'm more inspired to keep painting, but I don't want to keep my inspiration waiting on me.

On my way out I pass the room producing the loud music and stop to watch the artist in action. Instead of an easel, her canvas is on the ground. Steady strokes are replaced by erratic motions, tossing paint randomly on the canvas below her. From outside of the room I'm unable to see the actual art, but I'd be interested in seeing how it turns out. Before I turn I realize her paint is falling to the beat of the song playing throughout the room.

The receptionist, a man with a pin through his nose and pad locks hanging from his ears, is concentrating on the computer in front of him. "I'm all done," I say as I place my canvas on the floor in front of me.

"Let me grab your phone." One of the rules of the studio is to check in your phone before your session. They promote distraction free creativity. When he hands me my phone he says, "If you're interested, we have a monthly exhibit featuring art created here in the studio." With a pamphlet outstretched he says, "The next one is the last weekend of the month."

I tap a reminder in my phone and thank him on my way out of the door. The traffic on the return trip to Nicole's apartment solidifies the Atlanta traffic statistics. The longer I wait in the trail of cars, inching along the highway, the more I miss Tennessee. Taking a look out of the window, the lady creeping along the highway next to me makes eye contact. She smiles with her eyebrow cocked. I return her smile, and if it were any other time I may have even tried to persuade her to roll her window down so I could talk to her. Instead I smile back then turn to the road ahead of me.

Although traffic was thick, I beat Nicole home. Inside I find a nice spot for her to consider hanging my painting. Behind me I hear the door unlock and stand in front of the painting, blocking her view of it until I have time to tell her about it.

Chapter Sixteen

NICOLE

Bryan's broad body standing in my living room as the first thing I see after a boring day at work causes me to flash back to last night. When we gave up the effort of not having sex, and instead dived head first into a love making session, that was the absolute best way to break my curse and end my vagina's drought. "Hey there," I say as I drop my bag on my kitchen counter. Bryan maintains his position in the living room and I say, "Did you explore Atlanta today?" He nods his head.

I walk toward him and he reaches out for me. Closing our personal space, I look up at him and he smiles. As he rests his head on mine, I close my eyes and will time to stand still. I pull away before he does and I ask, "You cool?" He shakes his head and I continue, "Want to tell me about it?" After years of messing around with different guys, avoiding heartbreak by acting as if commitment wasn't a big deal to me, now to have a guy that I don't want to act with anymore is scary. Now that he's got the goods he could switch it up on me. All the affection and attention could come to a halt.

"I told you about the women I've painted in the past." I nod my head. "I painted you today." I step away from him and my eyebrows gather. One of his paintings is hanging on the bedroom wall of Mrs. Davenport's, the woman he had an affair with, hanging just above where she and her husband undoubtedly lay their heads at night, an odd revenge effort by Mrs. Davenport. "The studio I found here in the city was just what I needed today."

"Just like the others. I'm now immortalized on a canvas?" Bryan stares at me with his eyes squinted. "Not sure how I feel about that." Bryan steps aside and reveals the painting. I've seen his paintings before, but not in person, all images I scrolled through on his phone. The way he captured me in my sweats and headscarf, I can't describe. My mouth drops. "Bryan..."

"I didn't think about how me painting you would make you feel like the women who came before you." I sigh because although the painting, and his perception of me even while wearing sweats and a headscarf makes me feel like he sees more of me than just what he can get from me, I don't feel special. Him painting me isn't unique. Him painting me puts me into the group of all the women who came before me, the women he refused to settle down with. He grabs my chin and says, "Your thoughts are all over your face. Although I painted you, I don't view you as the others. I view us differently."

He closes his eyes then re-opens them, taking me by the wrist and guiding me to the couch. Instead of taking a seat beside him he pulls me onto his lap. Staring at the painting and examining each detail, I take note of the colors he chose, especially those woven through the headscarf. "Your memory is ridiculous." He shifts below me. "Thank you for the painting." Turning from the painting and making eye contact with Bryan I say, "But you're right, the gesture has me in an odd place."

"I'll tell you this. Those women may have received a painting from me, but that was it." He looks to my kitchen then back to me. "You're the first women I ever cooked for." Resting his hand on my thigh he says, "And you're definitely the only." He taps his finger where his hand rested. "Only woman I've ever wanted to wait with, to get to know, to not only want a sexual encounter with." I roll my eyes. "I know words alone don't carry much weight." I shrug my shoulders. "Let me show you."

Part of me wants to take Bryan to my bed and let him show me sexually, one last time, then dismiss this... this relationship or whatever it is we have going on. Part of me wants him to prove to me that he does want this, that I am different. "Okay," I finally mumble. "I'll let you show me."

He rakes his hand over my thigh before saying, "How about let's start with dinner. What do you usually eat during the week?"

Moving off his lap to sit beside him, I laugh. "You know I have no issue eating sketchy food." His eyes grow wide but he doesn't speak any objections. "If you weren't here I'd open my drawer full of menus and select a place that delivers. Not necessarily places I'd dine-in at, but decent food."

"You are determined to have me sitting on the toilet." My smile grows. "Don't you remember your last day in New York?" The food truck festival had me ailing, but Bryan jumped into action and brought me medicine.

"I haven't had any issues from the places I've ordered from." I walk to my drawer and grab a handful of menus. Bryan walks up behind me looking over my shoulder.

"How about that one?" He picks the Chinese takeout menu. "What do you order from there?"

"Sweet and sour chicken, and egg rolls." I turn to him with my eyebrows arched. "Do you want the same?"

"I should probably stick to the same; trying something

else may have me all messed up on the plane tomorrow." I stare at Bryan for a minute before he kisses my forehead. "I don't want to throw your whole week off, and I need to get home to find an art studio before rent is due." I laugh, knowing that Bryan's money issues are nothing like my money issues. I'm sure we could compare bank records and see a stark difference. "Next time I come, I'll make sure to plan it out with you."

"When do you plan to come back?" The time between now and the next visit will be a true test for me. I've woken up a sleeping monster and to tell her to wait patiently before she can have any more action will be torture.

"In a few weeks." He grabs a bottle of water from the refrigerator. Just about the only beverage I have besides wine and liquor. "Will that work for you?"

A few weeks is sooner than I expected, but I don't want to appear excited or disappointed. "I'll check my calendar and get back to you." Holding the menu up I say, "Let me grab my phone to order this food. Should probably give you enough time to get the food worked out before your flight tomorrow." I nudge him in the side. "What time is your flight?"

Grabbing his belly he says, "It's at noon." He takes his bottle of water back to the couch and sits across from the painting. "Think you want to hang it up?" Considering most of my art in the apartment is stock art from a random website, I'd be happy to replace it with a one of a kind piece, especially from my favorite artist.

With my finger in the air I speak into the phone, repeating our order of sweet and sour chicken and egg rolls. After hanging up, I walk into the living room to where he is sitting on the couch. The large, red rose ordaining the wall from the Decor Store isn't special. I point to it and say, "There, we can take that one down."

Bryan looks behind him and says, "You mean this one of

a kind blooming rose?" He stands beside me gazing at the canvas. "I'd hate to replace this piece of fine art."

"You're right. I should find it a new home, worthy of its presence." I look to him and say, "Think you can get it on the plane without someone trying to steal it from you?" Reaching for the painting he smiles and pulls it off the wall, placing it beside the couch. Gently he hangs my custom piece on the wall and I gasp.

"Who knew I needed a custom self-portrait in my apartment? It's gorgeous." I turn and wrap my arms around his waist. "Even if I was like the others, and this is your parting gift to me, I don't think I would be mad anymore." He laughs and slaps me on the butt. "Now I need to go get into an outfit similar to the one that inspired this painting." I walk toward my bedroom and say, "The delivery should be here soon. Can you answer the door when they get here?"

"Sure," he responds behind me. In my bedroom, I pull off my clothes and as promised, I shrug into a t-shirt and sweats. In the bathroom, I pull my hair back and tie my colorful scarf around my head then wash off my make-up. I gaze at myself in the mirror and smile at my fresh face status.

A few taps sound at my door and I listen as Bryan walks over. I forgot to give him the money. I walk to the kitchen and dig in my purse when I hear Bryan say, "My bad, you're here to see Nicole?" I drop my wallet when I hear the response from the guy at the door. Walking up behind Bryan I see Kevin standing in front of him.

"Hi, Kevin," I say and Bryan walks away leaving me to face Kevin.

"I was in the area and hadn't heard from you in a while." He looks behind me then says, "I should have called first."

I don't know how I should respond. Although Bryan isn't standing nearby I'm sure he's listening intently.

"Yeah." Biting my lip I continue, "Call you this weekend?"

He nods his head and turns to walk away but before he's out of sight he says, "I'll talk to you this weekend." I close the door softly and take my time turning around. Bryan isn't in the kitchen or the living room, but before I can make it to the bedroom, another knock at my door sounds. Grabbing my wallet, I open the door hoping this time I see the deliveryman.

With the bags in tow I walk toward the bedroom and tell Bryan the food has arrived. Bent over his luggage he looks at me and says, "On my way."

Plating the food, unlike I'd do if I were home alone, I set each of our plates at the counter and grab a bottle of wine and two glasses. "Wine with Chinese?"

"If you haven't had sketchy food with a glass of wine you have missed out," I say smiling.

"Maybe that's how you coat your stomach and prevent an onset of the shits." I burst out laughing. "I'm down if it's worked for you. Pour it out." We each take a couple of bites of the food without any words. Then Bryan sets his fork on his plate and says, "Is Kevin one of your dudes?"

Mimicking Bryan's actions I place my fork on my plate and say, "We've gone on a date before."

"Just one date," he asks with his eyebrows raised. I nod my head and he says, "Damn, it takes a dude with some huge balls to show up unannounced."

My eyes bulge and I shake my head in disbelief. "Are you talking about yourself or Kevin?" Considering Bryan surprised me just a day before without a call or plans, he must agree that his actions were bold.

Bryan cackles. "You're right." He tugs at his crotch. "I do have balls for showing up surprising you. Excuse me for feeling like I'm any different from any of your other dudes.

Glad I already planned to talk to you before popping up next time," he says sarcastically.

"Ah, sounds like you know how it feels to be in comparison with the others," I say with a smile. "Doesn't feel quite right to be lumped into that category, right?"

Bryan sucks in his lips, sending all types of hormonal signals off in my body. I'm trying to keep calm and have an adult conversation but my body is being petty wanting to just get in as much pleasure as I can before he leaves tomorrow. "It doesn't feel right." He looks at me. "For some reason it seems like we are both beyond that bucket of fuck buddies." He places both hands on the counter, spread apart. "Like we are over here." He looks at his right hand then to his left hand. "And they are over here. Miles apart."

I burst out laughing at his analogy. But it's spot on. When he revealed my custom painting, I felt like I was in the bottom of the barrel of fuck buddies. I felt like there was no chance of there being anything more than just the fucking. Although the fucking was good, and I would take that on a good day, this felt like it was more than just fucking. And if it wasn't more now, it would be more in the future. "But what now?"

I've been in relationships before. After the fuck dude who stole my virginity in high school, I thought I was in love in college. It happened fast; we met, and he wooed me, and just like that I was in a relationship. Soon after I was fighting the urge to tell him I loved him. Then, I had to return to Tallahassee for school, and he was in Georgia. At first, he would call, but after time that got old. I was back on campus with sexy guys shooting their best shot, and it didn't take long before I had no more will to ignore them. And just like that, I stopped answering his calls and it was over.

Looking at Bryan I shrug. "Guess we'll just see what

happens. If we can both handle this distance." I look at his hands that are still spread apart representing the bucket full of fuck buddies and us and say, "As long as the distance doesn't become too hard to bear where we have to go digging into the barrel maybe we can have a relationship."

Bryan grabs his stomach. "Think I should give up on this food. Don't think my stomach is ready for it yet." He pushes his plate away from him. He reaches for the wine but shakes his head rising from his chair. "I better wash all that down with some water."

My eyes squint together. "That was a quick reaction. Maybe my stomach really has hardened." With our plates in hand I move toward the kitchen. "Your last night in the area," I say.

"For a while," he says. With the water running I turn to him looking up to hear more. "My last night in the area for a while." He smiles. "I'll be back soon."

"Okay, so what do you want to do for the rest of the night?" He stands close behind me encasing me on both sides with his arms.

"I have a couple of thoughts." He kisses my neck and I'm excited we both have the same thoughts. "The art gallery first." Not what I was thinking. The spoon in my hand slips and clatters loudly against the sink. Bryan laughs and kisses my neck again. "We'll get to that too."

Chapter Seventeen

BRYAN

"That one makes me want to sing," I say looking at the picture of a street band with buckets flipped over as a set of drums.

Nicole looks up at me and asks, "Want to give me another rendition of the Clark Brothers?" I shake my head. "Maybe later?" Nicole sighs. "I need a creative talent. I actually don't think I have any."

Raising her hand to my mouth, I place a kiss on the back of it before saying, "You do. We all do. You just have to tap into it." Nicole shrugs and looks back at the piece displayed in front of us. The art gallery is displaying a local artist with a street artist theme. Although it's been a while since I've walked the streets of downtown Atlanta, from these pictures it appears not much has changed. Atlanta, like many cities, has a number of hustlers. Some selling knock-off purses, or jewelry, others displaying their talent for a tip.

"If it came down to it at least you could sell your art on the street."

"Yes, the streets of Atlanta. I think I may know

someone who may let me crash on her couch." Nicole nods her head. "Let's meet the artist."

The artist, a young female with hair as artistic as her paintings stands near one of her pieces. With a crowd gathered around listening to her describe the motivation for her pieces, Nicole and I stand waiting for them to thin out. When I get a closer look at her, I vaguely remember her face. Then the sound of music bursts through my thoughts.

The artist remains after the crowd clears and Nicole offers her hand first. "Beautiful work here." The artist shakes her hand and accepts Nicole's compliments. "Are you from Atlanta?"

"I am. You may have even passed me downtown one day. These street artists are my peers." Nicole cocks her head to the side. "Before getting into this gallery I was homeless. Then someone saw one of my pieces and offered me an opportunity and a place to stay."

"That's amazing," I say offering my hand. "I think I saw you earlier today." She looks at me without a sense of familiarity. "At the studio."

She nods. "I was out at the studio today. Hopefully, my music didn't bother you."

I shake my head and say, "No, it didn't bother me." I look around me and ask, "Did that piece make it here?"

"No, that's for a different gallery." She looks between Nicole and I and then asks, "Do you paint?"

"I do," I say. Nicole shakes her head. "Don't want to keep you too long." Another crowd starts to gather around us. "It was a pleasure meeting you." Nicole and I shake hands with the artist again before walking toward the exit.

"I feel like my walls could use another custom piece." We stop at the door and she says, "Especially since it would be going to support her." She looks back at the artist with her wild hair and knowing her passion is just as fierce as her hair, I can support Nicole's desire.

"Let's do it. Which one?"

Nicole puts her finger in the air and walks away. I stand at the exit flipping through my phone. When Nicole returns she says, "Alright. Ready."

We walk back to the car hand in hand and the chill of the night causes Nicole to walk closer to my side. "I love the fall weather," I say wrapping an arm around her shoulders.

"I bet you do. It's prime cuddle weather," Nicole says with a laugh.

"Football season actually. I've never been big on cuddling."

Nicole gasps. "Football? Over cuddling?" She snuggles even closer and says, "I'm ready to teach you to fall in love with cuddling."

"I won't complain."

On our drive home, we notice a few street performers and both Nicole and I point them out as we pass. "If there is one thing that's sure about black folks, it's that they know how to come up in life. Always hustling, never afraid to use their talents." I notice Nicole's face downturn and I ask, "What do you really love to do in your spare time?" She looks at me with a deviant grin and I say, "Besides that."

"Oh, I like reading. I love talking, joking around." She looks at me with her eyes pulled together. "Why?"

"Sometimes your talent is hidden in the things you love to do."

"Interesting." For the remainder of the ride we listen to the music and although my ears are on the lyrics, I'm sure Nicole is lost in her thoughts, resting on the armrest between us with her finger on her chin.

When we pull up to her apartment I open her door and reach for her hand, wrapping my fingers between hers. "Now on to your other favorite past time," I say with my eyebrow raised.

Nicole says, "That's what I'm talking about."

As soon as the door closes behind us Nicole pulls her shirt over her head and throws it to the floor. Following behind her I watch as each piece of her clothing is thrown off in the same manner. I stand and watch as she stretches across her bed completely naked. "What are you waiting for?" she asks.

"Guess I was captivated by the sight in front of me." I begin throwing my clothes off with less fanfare. My shoes, shirt, and pants land in a pile near the bed.

With her head hoisted up by her hand Nicole looks at me and says, "And those?" I look down at my boxers and shrug out of those too. She smiles wide before I climb into the bed beside her.

With both of us naked and shivering under her cold air, we pull the blanket back and crawl beneath the sheets. Just as she led us here, I let her take lead in the bed. With her eyes fluttering beneath her long lashes, she leans into me and reaches behind my head. Her kisses are slow and deliberate. I return the momentum, tasting her lips beneath my tongue. With her chest against mine, I rub her back and she deepens our kiss.

After a tug to my shoulders I'm laying on top of her, breaking our kiss to spread the love down her body. Kisses to her neck and chest, and down her happy trail to her most sensitive spot. When I kiss all around it she begins to squirm. I end her squirming with a kiss to her spot, savoring my first taste of her. I hear her moan and her body stiffens.

I continue getting to know each crevice of her body before I feel her release. Then I look up to her and ask, "Do you have any condoms around here?" I remembered that the one we used last night was my last. She nods her head and points toward her bedside table. I rise from the bed and rummage through the drawer, past her mini vibrator and below a stack of papers I find a few condoms. Grabbing one and rolling it on, I climb back into place over her body.

She takes my face in her hands and pulls me in for a kiss, quicker and more fervent than the one before, and we kiss as I enter her. A sensation washes over me and I fight the urge to reach my release before we're ready, before she's ready to succumb to another wave of pleasure. Her nails dig into my back and her teeth graze my neck, and without her saying it I know her body is growing weak.

I draw back and slowly re-enter her, until I feel her quiver, until she says, "Bryan" in my ear, and when she does I have no more resolve. I release. With my eyes closed tight I roll to the side of Nicole and she finds her place beside me, just how we started, side by side, with her curves fitting neatly into mine.

Drifting into sleep I hear Nicole when she leaves the bed headed toward the bathroom. A nudge to my side wakes me again. "Hey, I need to do some work. I'll be in the living room," she says. I nod my head without opening my eyes, but after she leaves the room sleep evades me. Being here, I feel like I've cracked the code that Nicole had hidden away. The code that would let me in, but I remember what she said earlier about distance. Can I handle the distance?

Before leaving for Tennessee, my New York apartment was beginning to feel homey. Not like home, but I was becoming comfortable in the space. Now that I'm back from Tennessee, and especially Atlanta, my apartment feels cold.

My paintings that I sent back with Chris are on the ground sitting against the walls with my supplies in heaps in a corner. Unlike my condo in Knoxville, I don't have a room to set up as a studio. I'll have to move all this, hopefully to a place nearby. With my newest piece of art in hand I search for my hammer. The red rose doesn't match anything in my apartment, but I'll make it work.

Pounding my hammer against the nail on the corner wall of my bedroom feels right. Having Nicole's art in my room feels right. If nothing else, I'll be reminded of her before I go to bed at night and when I wake up every morning. As an artist, if anyone visits, hopefully they don't see this stock piece in my house and question my artistic judgment. With the picture hanging, I step back and snap a picture to send to Nicole.

Bryan: *Doesn't look too bad in its new home.*

I didn't tell Nicole that I was bringing the picture with me to New York. She may not have even noticed when she got home that the picture was missing. Now on to my actual art, I need to find homes for each of these pieces. Sitting on the couch, I use my phone to search for nearby studios to continue painting and to display my finished art. Finding one about two blocks away, I give them a call and set up a meeting.

Standing, I shift through each of the pieces on the ground and make sure I have pictures of them in my phone when I see a piece I've already mentally given away. A piece I thought would be the perfect gift for her. I pull it out of the stack and set it aside. My phone dings with a message back from Nicole and I smile when I see no words but the portrait from the gallery of the street performers, those who were banging on the buckets.

Bryan: *Great choice. Need help hanging it?*

Chris should be home by now, and I owe him a visit. I'm sure he's missed me over the last few days. With my keys and phone in hand, I leave out of the apartment to catch up with him.

"Damn, dude. Finally back," Chris says as he holds the door open.

"Yeah, you busy?"

Chris moves out of the way and lets me in the apartment. "No, just got off. Waiting for Laila to get home so we can grab dinner." The routine was familiar for me, for a day, a routine I could take on more regularly. "How was your surprise trip?" Chris laughs and plops on his couch as he removes his shoes. "I assume since your ass wasn't back here on Sunday that she didn't kick you out for showing up unannounced."

"It was a good visit. She was pleasantly surprised." I sit down on the couch beside him. "Next time I'll plan the trip with her though." Thinking of old dude showing up without calling made me feel territorial, but it also put me in my place.

"Oh yeah, mister dick slayer, finally realized that women aren't waiting for you to arrive?"

"Man look. I'm trying to change my ways."

Chris drops his shoe on the ground beside him. Looking at me with his eyebrows raised he says, "Y'all fucked?"

My head falls back on his couch and I laugh. Of course he takes me wanting to change my ways as we fucked. "All in my business." I smirk at him. "Unrelated, I may need your help with moving the art from my apartment to a studio."

"Yeah it was a challenge getting it all into your apartment. Just let me know when you're ready."

"Thanks. I appreciate it." I slap his leg and say, "When my art starts selling for millions I won't forget about you."

The door opens and Chris and I both look toward it waiting for Laila to walk through. She puts her bag down, with her phone to her ear she looks up to both of us and smiles widely. Hurrying off the phone, she comes over to the both of us and gives Chris a kiss before wrapping her arms around me. "I was just starting to miss you." She squeezes onto the couch between me and Chris. "How was Tennessee?"

Although I'm sure she'd rather hear about my trip to see her friend, I follow her questioning. "It was a good trip. Always good to be back home. Driving my car, no traffic, the folks, good food." I look at her with a wide smile after realizing I miss home more than I let myself believe. "It was good."

Chris nods his head in agreement. "I'd agree to all of that." He rubs Laila's leg and says, "Next time you have to join us." She sighs and agrees.

"Yeah, Mom was disappointed to only have us boys home." My mom is still chomping at the bit for a daughter-in-law. Chris is the closest to delivering on that request.

"Don't want to disappoint momma," Laila says.

"Nope." As trained robots Chris and I say in unison, "Don't ever want to disappoint Mom."

Laila laughs at our rendition of my dad's favorite catch phrase. No matter how much he judged us for our recklessness, or scolded us for our decisions, Mom was the good cop. We were raised to believe making her the bad cop would be the ultimate indiscretion.

"And how was your surprise, last minute, unplanned, trip to Atlanta?" Laila leaves no room for me to misunderstand her thoughts of my trip to Atlanta.

I face her with her eyebrows raised and her arms crossed her chest. "Tell me how you really feel." She begins to speak then stops. "It was a good trip." I turn my head sideways to judge her reaction. "Did you hear otherwise?"

"Nope. Just got a mini cursing out for giving you Nicole's address."

"It was all to the good. I think I'll go back, planned, totally not random, with Nicole in on all the plans, at the end of the month."

"That good, huh?" She slaps my knee. "I'm happy to hear it. You both deserve a good person in your lives." She's right, we both deserve to be happy.

"Let me get out of here." I stand to leave and walk toward the door. "I'll catch up with y'all later." Looking over my shoulder with the door held open I tell Chris, "As soon as I have the details on the studio I'll give you a call for your help."

Being alone in my apartment feels strange. A few days of having at least one person around me at all times was comforting. Sitting on the couch, I scroll through my phone for the address to send the art I had set aside. I heard she returned to her childhood home, moving in after her father passed away. I haven't seen her in a while, and have no plans of seeing her again. But she, more than anyone else, needs this piece of art.

Chapter Eighteen
NICOLE

"Are you sure your dude won't be upset if we are out together?" I love it when a guy passively asks if I'm single. I look up at Kevin and roll my eyes softly. After he came to my apartment unannounced and bumped into Bryan I'm sure he thinks I'm in a relationship. Hell, I'd think I were in a relationship too, had I been him.

"You can ask me straight up, no need to beat around the bush." I turn to the window and watch the people strolling past.

Kevin taps the table and says, "I apologize." I look back at Kevin and my mouth nearly falls open. I don't think I've ever had a guy apologize. For anything. "That's offensive to assume that you would be out with me if you had a guy. That you would have let me approach you in the grocery store that day."

I shrug my shoulders. "You're right. If I did have a dude, I would hope I'd respect him enough to not be out around town with you or anyone else." Shuffling my rice around my plate with my fork I say, "I'm single. I have been for a while."

"I know it's cliché`, but why?" Kevin asks with a stone face. "You're gorgeous, with a good sense of humor, slightly sarcastic, and you're independent. Has to be by choice, right?"

"Thanks for all of that." I cock my head and smile. "Except for the sarcastic piece. You could have kept that to yourself." Kevin laughs and his smile... that damn smile. It's an automatic panty dropper, making me shift in my seat. "It is by choice. Maybe when I find a guy who is serious about being in a relationship it'll happen."

He nods his head. He looks down at my plate and says, "Looks like you are finished with your food. Ready to go?" When I called Kevin yesterday, he asked if we could grab lunch and visit the Botanical Gardens today. Not having much else to do today I agreed. It's been years since I've been to the Botanical Gardens, and from what I remember it's a neat experience.

"Yeah let's go check out this garden." After Kevin pays, we walk back to his car to drive the short distance.

When we enter the gardens, Kevin reaches for my hand and we walk hand and hand through the floral exhibits, stopping to admire the different floral sculptures and flower exhibits. Kevin speaks to some of the employees in passing, and initially I think it's his southern hospitality. But then I realize his level of familiarity exceeds just a simple 'hello.' "Do you know them?" I ask after we pass a few employees who stop and speak to Kevin about the new exhibit on the other side of the garden.

"Something like that." He leads me in the direction of the new exhibit. With Fall as its theme, the pumpkins and orange orchids are gathered to create a display worthy of Halloween. Beside the exhibit is a bench under a fully bloomed tree, the perfect spot for shade. He nods toward the bench and asks, "Want to take a seat?"

"Sure." After walking around most of the garden my

feet could use a break. "What type of work do you do?" When we first met, I didn't have high hopes for seeing Kevin too often. I kept our conversation light. Didn't ask many questions about his life.

"I run a non-profit for young men." He turns his body on the bench to face me. Swiping at the sweat that had pooled around his neck he continues, "Not what I intended to do when I graduated but it's the most satisfying job I've ever had." He smiles and I know he's genuine about his response.

"Did you start the non-profit?" Although the shade is blocking the sun, the heat is unforgiving. I feel like I'm back in Tallahassee in the middle of summer. I pluck at my shirt to keep it from sticking to my skin.

"No, I didn't start it. It's been around for many years. The founder is older and wanted to start transitioning leadership before he couldn't contribute to the direction after his departure." I nod my head as he describes his role, and the goals of the organization.

I disrupt him and say, "You're really passionate about your work."

He sighs and says, "After all these years. I really am. Enough about me. What is it that you do?"

I roll my eyes, not at him but at the thought of my day job. "I majored in business. Such a generic major, and my job is nothing I thought I'd be doing." Kevin bites his lip. "Nothing I'm passionate about but it fits its purpose. Paychecks are reliable." Shrugging I say, "Of course I'd love to be able to go on and on about my job the way you did and feel the joy you just expressed, but I just need to discover what it is that will fill that spot for me."

Kevin puts his arm around my shoulders and, unlike before, I don't feel a sexual attraction to him. Feels like I'm sitting here with a good friend, not someone I'm trying to get into bed with. Not someone who could scratch this itch that I'm sure will return at the exact point when I have nobody around. What's going on with me? I'm tempted to touch my head and check for a temperature. "At least you recognize you want a change and you know you have work to do to figure it out."

My head sways side to side. "Yeah." I sigh. "Are you from here?" I ask leaning away from his arm to look at him as he answers.

"No, I'm not from Atlanta. Or Georgia." Kevin stills and instead of telling me where he's from he asks, "You?"

"Yes, I'm from Georgia. Born and raised. But growing up I lived outside of the city." Before I can dig more into his story, a few kids run past us screaming, and our quiet moment is gone.

Kevin watches the kids run in front of us while their mom attempts to chase after them. When the mom loses, Kevin hops out of his seat and outstretches his hand to me. "There are a couple of other cool exhibits we should see before we leave today."

I try to ignore my phone vibrating in my purse, but the persistence of the person calling is unwavering. I tug Kevin toward an exhibit with burgundy and burnt orange flowers. Leaning against the gate, I dig my phone out of my purse and shake my head when I see Big Daddy flashing on the screen. Before I can stuff my phone back into my purse Kevin asks, "Need to take that?"

"No, it can wait." I turn to the flowers and try to distract Kevin from the phone call. "I'm pretty sure that Fall is my favorite season." Although the heat today feels nothing like fall. "Actually, I love Fall when it feels like Fall." I look at the sweat accumulating on Kevin's forehead in small beads. "Damn global warming and all."

"Right," He says as he wipes at his forehead again. Unable to catch each bead of sweat he leans on the gate beside me and says, "It's my second favorite. Spring would definitely be my first. A fresh beginning, decent weather that breaks the horrible winter."

"Horrible winter?" I say in a high-pitched tone. "In Georgia?"

"Winter in Georgia is weak. But it's still cold and dreary, dark most of the day." Kevin reaches for my hand and asks, "Are you ready to get out of here?" I nod my head. "Your favorite season isn't being as kind to us." Walking out of the gardens Kevin asks, "Do you have plans for the rest of your day?"

Bryan and I didn't commit to being in a relationship, or not seeing other people, but we did say we'd see what would happen. I told Kevin I was single, and that's true. Kinda. I mean if Bryan called me and told me that he was on a date today I'd think his willpower to sustain the distance was not successful. I'd jump to all sort of conclusions about this thing we are doing being pointless. "I have a few errands I need to run." I'd lie and say I needed to go grocery shopping but I couldn't say that with a straight face.

"I know how that can be. The week is busy. Just when we thought the weekend was supposed to be filled with fun, adulthood rained on us like the plague."

I chuckle to myself because that reality couldn't be further from the truth. "Wise words."

"If only it weren't true." He opens my car door and I climb in, thankful for the seat. "If you aren't busy next weekend I hope we can spend some time together." He looks at me as he straps in his seat belt. "You know, between adulting."

Instead of verbally responding, I nod my head, but mentally consider how I'll avoid his calls next week. For the first time, since I don't know when, I don't want multiple guys on my bench. I don't feel like I need a backlist of guys to call when I need some loving. Bryan better deliver on his trip at the end of the month. If not, I'll be kicking myself for this empty bench I'll have.

Instead of running errands I look around my small apartment and decide to start cleaning. Although I don't cook, I do clean. While I'm wiping my counter my phone rings and I dig through my purse to grab it. "Jennifer," I yell into the mouthpiece before putting it on speaker to continue wiping the counter. "How are you?"

Jennifer laughs then says, "I'm good. Haven't heard from you east coast chicks in a while." Jennifer's right, I haven't called her in a while and we are way overdue for a trip. But unless she's opening her pocketbook to come visit me, it'll be next year before I have some spare change for another plane ticket. "What have you been up to? And why am I on speaker?"

"You're on speaker because I'm in the middle of cleaning my house. I haven't been up to much. I went out with a friend today."

"Oh my, tell me more." Jennifer and I were very close our freshman year of college. We stayed in the same small dorm room together, and our second year we moved out to an apartment where Laila and Monica joined us. I love Jennifer, but she strongly opposed me mingling with different dudes and it didn't take long before I'd avoid her. "Was this just another guy or is this a potential boyfriend?"

"It's our second time out together." I laugh and say, "And you'd be happy to know we haven't had sex." Jennifer gasps.

"Am I talking to a changed Nicole?" The sarcasm laced in her voice causes me to roll my eyes.

"It's nothing serious. What's going on with you and your boyfriend?" I ask focusing the attention back to her.

"He's still around," she sighs, "After moving in together I don't know what I expected to happen, but whatever I expected hasn't happened."

Throughout our years at L. U. Jennifer went on very few dates. Rightfully so, she didn't trust many guys. When she met Derrick, she surprised us all when they became inseparable senior year. "Have the flames burned out?" I hear old people say that all the time. After some time of being with the same person you have to keep rekindling the flame.

"I guess you can say that. We have our routine, and I don't know."

"Sounds like y'all need to shake it up a bit. You still want to be with him, right?" My phone dings with an incoming call and I look at the screen and see Big Daddy, again.

"I do want to be with him. I couldn't imagine being with anyone else. But I guess being an adult isn't as thrilling as our college years." My laughter echoes through the apartment. "Or maybe it's just me."

"Oh no honey. I'm sitting here on a Saturday, after a day date, cleaning my apartment. This adult life is nothing to brag about." My phone dings again and I say, "Do you remember Chris' brother Bryan?" When she doesn't respond affirmatively I say, "He came down a couple of times while Chris was on campus. When I was up visiting Laila, he was there."

"Wait, I think I know where this is going. You fucked Laila's brother-in-law?"

"Brother-in-law... girl. No, we didn't fuck in New York. But we kept in touch, and he surprised me with a visit here in Atlanta."

"He surprised you with a visit?" The excitement in her voice returns. "Sounds kinda serious."

"I think he wants to be serious, but..."

"Nicole, I get it. You have lived life footloose and care-free for years, avoiding commitment at all costs." I nod my head cause Jennifer is absolutely right. "But if I can settle down and trust Derrick, then I know you can. If Bryan is a good dude I think you should give it a try." She laughs. "Tell dude who took you on a date today it was nice but don't keep him around."

"Oh, Jennifer. When did you become so wise?"

She cackles. "I've always been wise. You just didn't want to hear any of my antics." She's definitely right about that because in college, anything she said or offered up on my personal life was ignored. "I need to go find Derrick. As I've been sitting here, I realize we need to liven it up a bit. I'm going to pull on a sexy dress and we're going on a date."

"Get it girl! Have fun." After hanging up I finish cleaning my kitchen and grab a glass of wine. A call to Bryan is going to need some liquid courage.

With my legs propped up on the coffee table, my phone to my ear, and my glass of wine in my hand I listen as Bryan's phone goes straight to voicemail. I hate when people call you but don't answer when you call back.

Nicole: Call me when you can.

Chapter Nineteen
BRYAN

The sterile white walls and smell of disinfectant is making my time sitting in the waiting room intolerable. I stand to take a walk to the cafeteria, again. Between the five of us, the coffee and snacks have been flowing and will probably continue until he's out of surgery. "Anyone want anything from the cafeteria?" I ask.

My mother looks at me, her face weary, and says, "Baby, I think we've had plenty." She looks at my brothers and says, "Maybe you all should go home and rest for a bit."

I hold my hand up and say, "Absolutely not. Ma, we aren't leaving you here alone. I just need to take a walk." She nods and leans back in her seat. "I'll walk down to the cafeteria. Call me if you need me."

I thought the day I walked away from the family business was tough, but getting the phone call from my mother yesterday telling me that my father had a heart attack broke me. Chris, Laila, and I hopped on the first available flight from New York and we've been at the hospital since we landed.

Before I could even gather my thoughts the first person I tried calling, multiple times, was Nicole. When she didn't answer, I gave myself a reality check. We aren't in a relationship. Still seeing where this thing is going doesn't give me unfettered access to her.

"Bryan, let's go outside. The fresh air would be good for us." David places his arm around my shoulder and we walk toward the hospital exit. "I wish Mom would have come with me. She refuses to leave the waiting room."

"Dad has to be okay, man. What will she do if something happens?"

David closes his eyes, re-opening them with moisture present. "I don't want to think about what any of us will do without that man." We find a bench near the entrance and take a seat.

I shake my head. "I'm glad the last time I was home we had a good conversation, but had I known it could have been my last time with him I would have stayed longer. I would have soaked in his wisdom."

"Hindsight is twenty-twenty. It's times like these when people realize they have to slow down and live in the moment." David hits his knee. "Whatever happens we have to move forward with that goal." He wipes at his face. "I just hope we have more time with him."

"If only we could control time." Leaning back on the bench, I let myself rest with the air clearing my mind. David and I sit side-by-side until his phone begins to ring. He walks away to take the call.

David sighs and I look up at him, with the sun shining brightly behind him, I have to squint my eyes to see his face. "Word got out to the staff at the firm. That was Reese, asking if we needed anything." David rubs his face where his stubble is growing. "What will we do at the firm if something happens to Dad?"

"You and Chris will be able to pull it together." Even without my dad, I have no intentions of returning to the family business. "But let's not think about that."

My phone dings alerting me of a text message and I pause when I see Chris' name. I'm sure if he had bad news he would have called and not sent a text message. I take a long breath before reading the message.

Chris: You should come back to the waiting room.

"That's Chris. He says we should get back to the waiting room." David follows behind me as I walk briskly through the halls of the hospital. When I see her sitting next to my mom I look from her to Chris and mouth to him, "What's she doing here?" Chris' eyebrows raise and he shakes his head. "Shelby?"

Shelby places her hand on my mom's knee and looks at me. "Bryan." Neither of us make any moves.

"How did you know we were here?" Seeing Shelby sitting amongst my family doesn't anger me as I would have expected. My mouth forms into a smile, maybe for the first time since we rushed to the hospital.

Shelby turns to my mom and whispers to her before rising to stand in front of me. "It didn't take long for the news to spread about your father, Bryan. He's respected here. The entire city is praying he pulls through."

With my hands stuffed in my pockets to avoid touching her, I look for an empty set of chairs. "Let's take a seat." Shelby follows behind me to the chairs in the corner of the room.

"Your mother said you all are still waiting on the doctors to give you news on the surgery." I nod my head. "I asked her if you all needed anything. I can imagine what y'all are going through." Shelby lost her father years ago and although we weren't together at the time, my mom kept me posted. After he passed away she moved back in with her mother. "The waiting is the worst."

"It is." It's worse than the waiting I endured after Shelby and I broke up in college. I waited thinking she'd change her mind. Thinking that she'd rally behind my goals and aspirations to leave college and become an artist. Thinking she'd get over the idea of us being the perfect couple, me working for the family business and she working for a local law firm. I waited for a few weeks, then months, then finally I gave up. Today I'm not giving up on my dad; today I'll wait till he comes out of surgery; till the doctor comes into the waiting room and gives us good news. I'll wait till he's fully recovered. I'll stay here in Tennessee and wait till he returns to the firm, better than he left.

"Bryan," Shelby places her hand over mine sitting on the armrest. "Thank you for the art you sent." I sent the art to prove to her that she shouldn't have dismissed my dreams. I sent it to her to prove had we stayed together we could have still been that perfect couple. I sent it to her to be a reminder that you should follow your dreams and not give up on them. I didn't send it to her for anything more than that.

"You're welcome." I don't want Shelby to think she owes me anything. "Thanks for coming by."

Shelby looks at me before standing. With her hand on my shoulder she says, "Let me know if you need anything." She turns to leave and I watch her walk out of the waiting room. Before my mind can drift into the what-if scenarios I sit beside my mother.

"Patience is a virtue that is escaping me today." One day I'd love to have a woman as virtuous as my mother. Her patience with my father and us boys over the years has been nothing short of amazing.

"Ma, you haven't even left this seat since we've been here." I wrap my hand around hers. "You have the patience of Job." She smiles and although it only lasts for a second it brings a smile to my face.

"Oh, Bryan. This is the ultimate test." Her eyes grow wide and I follow her gaze to the entrance. The doctor in his blue scrubs and white jacket walks toward us.

With his hand outstretched my mother takes it in hers and I wrap my arm around her. We both stay seated side-by-side with my brothers gathering around us. "The surgery went well. We were able to implant the stent and his artery appears to be responding." My mother's shoulders shudder and she begins to sob. "He should be out of recovery within the hour and you can go in to visit him."

My mom sniffles. "Thank you, doctor."

David walks with the doctor out of the waiting room. Chris and I stay with my mom and let her release all her tears. Once the floodgate is open the tears continue to flow.

Laila hands me a cup of water and I place it in my mom's hand. "Here Mom, take a sip." My mom takes a few sips and hands me the cup. "As soon as they let us in the room we'll go check on Dad."

Laila starts pacing back and forth and I stand, leaving the seat for Chris to take. "Laila, are you okay?"

Laila looks back at my mom and I follow her into the hallway. "I didn't realize how much this reminded me of my mom being in the hospital until now." She looks up the hallway. "When the doctor walked in I was reminded of how I felt waiting for the doctor to give us news about her."

I close my eyes and imagine how much harder today would be if it was my mom in surgery instead of my dad. "This is taxing on all of us."

"Being in the hospital with any family member is never easy." Laila leans against the wall. "After you all are able to see him, I'd recommend you all take turns getting a break away from here." I don't agree because I'm not sure I'll be able to leave after I see my dad, especially if my mom decides to stick around."

Laila twirls her phone between her hands. "I'm glad you were able to come down with Chris. I'm sure you being here is easing his stress," I look from her phone to her eyes, "even if only a little."

A slight smirk forms on Laila's face. "And looks like you had someone looking out for you too."

Shrugging off her reference to Shelby I say, "The last person I wanted to see, honestly."

"Who was she?" Laila whispers as if she was unsure if her question was appropriate.

"My ex from college." Laila's eyes grow wide. "First time I've seen her since we broke up."

"Wow. I bet that was awkward."

"Not as awkward as I had imagined." A nurse approaches us and slows as she nears the waiting room entrance.

"Are you all here for Mr. Clark?" I nod my head. "If you come with me, a couple of you can come back to visit him." I put my hand in the air and enter the waiting room to inform my mom.

Laila takes a seat near Chris and I walk with my mom behind the nurse. Instead of going inside with her, I give her a few minutes to speak with my dad. From the window I see her take his hand and lean into his ear. With his eyes half-open, he watches my mom but his mouth doesn't move.

When my mom takes a seat near the bed I walk into the room and take his free hand. His head turns toward my direction and I say, "Old man, you can't scare us like that." He doesn't respond verbally, but I feel his hand squeeze mine just a little tighter.

Although I don't want to leave him, I'm sure David and Chris are eager to lay eyes on him. I pat his hand and tell my mom I'll send them back. On my way to the waiting room I'm tempted to call Nicole again, but decide against it. Now is the time my family needs me, and I'll be here for them.

Chapter Twenty
NICOLE

Yesterday he was blowing up my phone and now he won't answer. Petty. With my hair wrapped and my baggy sweats on, I take a seat on the couch and flip through the channels. Last time I sat like this he showed up, and I would love for him to show up now, but he won't even answer the phone. Maybe he's done with me, maybe he's had a change of heart, and working this thing out is no longer his goal.

I stop flipping the channels when I see black women arguing on the screen. Diving into someone else's drama always clears my mind. My phone rings and my breath stills. I let it ring as I avoid looking at the screen. "Hello."

"Nicole, what are you doing?" Her voice is soft and she sounds exhausted.

"Sitting here watching television. My Sunday routine." I lower the television volume to hear Laila speak. "Are you okay?"

"I'm in Tennessee." In Tennessee? Laila only has one reason to be in Tennessee, and the same reason she has to be in Tennessee would probably put Bryan in Tennessee.

"Is everything okay?" My hand lays over my chest hoping to still my heart's fast pace.

"Mr. Clark." I gasp waiting for her to tell me the worst possible news I could hear. Maybe that's why Bryan was calling and no longer is answering his phone. Dammit. "He had a heart attack, and had surgery yesterday. He's recovering, but he hasn't been able to speak since he's been out of the surgery." Laila sniffles.

"Oh my goodness. How's the family?" Of course I'm worried about Bryan's mother, and his brothers, but mostly I'm worried about him.

"They are having a hard time right now. I was headed back to New York this evening but I've rescheduled my flight."

If Laila misses work I know it's something serious. "Do you need anything?"

"I haven't been able to get any of them to leave the hospital. They've been taking turns sitting up with Mr. Clark. Sitting in the waiting room is starting to take a toll on me, but they've had plenty of people coming in with food and snacks."

"I'm coming."

"Coming to Tennessee?" Laila stutters. "I can't ask you to do that, Nicole."

"You didn't ask, Laila. I offered." Hopping off the couch to find my work laptop I turn it on in preparation to send an email to my manager and one to Krista who will have to cover my meetings. "I'll call you when I'm on my way." Then it dawns on me, I need an address and should probably figure out how long it will take me to get to them. "Wait. Laila, text me the address of the hospital." She agrees and we hang up.

I walk between the bedroom and the living room a couple of times before I actually accomplish anything. A road trip to Tennessee to sit in the waiting room with a man's family who I've never met. This could turn out to be a terrible situation. What if Bryan needs space? If nothing else, I'll be there for Laila.

Grabbing my weekender bag, I throw in a couple of shirts and pants, and my necessities to stay hygienic as much as I can in a hospital waiting room. I stand in the middle of my room and try to think about other things I may need, but come up blank. I don't bother changing clothes since I'll be traveling for a few hours.

On my way to my car I call my parents to let them know I'm going on a road trip. "Nicole, hey baby. How are you?" I'm sure my mom is walking out of church where she prayed hard for me to return with them one day. At least that's what she'll tell me. "We missed you in church today."

"I hope it was a good service. If Daddy preached, I'm sure he delivered the word." Growing up as a preacher's kid, I stayed in church on Sundays, and throughout the week. After all those years, I learned to have a personal relationship with the Lord and decided I didn't need to be amongst His people in the church house. At least that's how I've convinced myself.

"Oh yes, dear. He preached the word today. Are you coming by for Sunday dinner?" As much as I love to eat my mama's cooking, like the church house, I've avoided my parent's house on Sundays. Feels like a mini church service with many of the church members visiting for a good meal and fellowship.

"Not today mama. I was actually calling to tell you I am taking a road trip."

"A road trip. On a Sunday, where are you going?"

"My friend's father had a heart attack. It's actually Laila's boyfriend's father. She's there at the hospital and I'm going to check on them."

"I'll be praying for his father, Nicole. I'll also be praying for your safety. Be careful on the road and call me as soon as you arrive." I didn't expect anything less from my mom. She's always been supportive of my decisions, even if deep down she may think I'm half crazy. Now had I called my dad, he would have told me to sit my butt down and pray. He would have told me to stay off the highway. I won't be surprised if he calls after my mom shares the news with him. But by then hopefully I'll be half way to Tennessee.

When I hang up with my mom I start my car and say a prayer, one for me and one for Mr. Clark.

Chapter Twenty-One
BRYAN

It's Chris' turn to relieve me from the bedside. We've been rotating every couple of hours to keep an eye on my mom who refuses to leave my dad. Her eyes have nodded off a few times since I've been sitting here and I wish my dad would wake long enough to tell her he's going to be okay, to tell her to go home and rest. Our only interaction with him has been to watch the machine that's been pumping oxygen into his body. He's taken a terrible turn since leaving surgery, and I hang my head as I leave his side; each time I leave I am reminded it could be the last.

"She needs to get some real sleep before she ends up sick." Chris looks beyond me as we pass each other through the door of my dad's room. "We don't need both of them in the hospital."

Looking back at my mom I nod my head. "The nurses have even offered her the shower down the hall to freshen up, but she won't move."

"Alright man." Chris pats my back and I leave the room. "I can stay longer if you want to go home and get some rest. David went to the office to send emails to the staff."

"I'll be okay." I continue down the hall to the waiting room. I rub my eyes and blink a few times. Exhaustion must be setting in because the woman I see walking my direction strongly resembles Nicole. I shake my head but the image doesn't refine itself. The woman stops walking and watches as I approach her.

"Nicole?" When I'm in front of her there is no denying what I see. My mind isn't playing tricks on me. She's here. I reach out for her hand. "When did you get here?"

She looks down at our hands. "I just pulled up a few minutes ago." She starts to speak again but stops with her mouth slightly open. I have an urge to take her lips in mine and kiss her, show her how much I appreciate her being here. But instead I remove my hand from hers.

"Thank you for coming, but you didn't have to drive all the way here." She steps back and looks me in the eyes.

"I don't want to be in the way. But when I talked to Laila, I wanted to be here." Of course, Laila is here. I look into the waiting room and see Laila sitting up in a chair with her head stretched, leaning against the wall.

"Right. Maybe you two can head to my parent's house. Let Laila get some rest." I walk over to Laila and nudge her arm. "You should go lay down. If we all end up sick, we won't be any help around here." Laila nods her head. I look at Nicole who is standing an arm's length away from me. "And after your drive you should get some rest too." I dig through my pocket for my keys. My parent's key has remained on this ring since childhood.

Handing the key to Nicole I let my hand linger in hers before saying, "Whatever you do, don't lose it. I'll text you the address."

"Thanks." Nicole places the key in her pocket before wrapping her arm around Laila and helping her out of the seat.

"Tell Chris I'll be back in a few hours. Let me know if

y'all need anything while we're gone." As they walk out of the door Laila looks at me. "Maybe I'll bring pillows." She twists her neck around.

Taking a new seat in the waiting room, by myself I look around and realize we were the only family in the waiting room. Usually the waiting room has other families waiting on their loved ones, but I'm glad others aren't going through what we are going through right now. I wouldn't wish this pain on my worst enemy.

Instead of resting my head against the wall, like Laila, I manage to rest my head in my lap. Sleep has escaped me since we've been back in Knoxville, but I let my eyes rest and my breathing slows.

"How long have you been asleep?" I sit up in my chair and blink my eyes as I try to focus on the person interrupting my sleep. I look around the room at the sterile walls, the medical signage, and realize I'm sitting in the waiting room. It wasn't a dream.

"I don't even know. How long have you been gone?" David looks at his watch and hunches his shoulders.

"I don't remember when I left." He sits beside me and asks, "Do you need to go to the house and get some rest?" His lips curl into a smile. "Or maybe get in a quickie."

I squint my eyes at David. "What are you talking about?"

"I had to go let your girl in the house. They set the alarm off."

"Oh shit. I forgot to tell her the code to the alarm." I shake my head. "Why didn't she call me?"

"Guess they couldn't reach you. Laila called Chris and he called me cause he didn't want to leave." David leans back in the chair looking for a comfortable position. "I was able to give them the code before the cops showed up, then I stopped by on my way back here to make sure they were okay." I stand up to stretch. David looks up at me with the same goofy smile. "Your girl is bad. Even with her hair wrapped up and those baggy clothes on." He trails off and I feel some type of way about him describing Nicole like some random chick on the street.

"Yo, dude, chill with all that." He throws his hands in the air. "I can't believe she drove here."

David shifts in his seat. "You mean you didn't know she was coming?" He nods his head then says, "Laila's idea?"

"I don't know whose idea it was but I don't need her here as a distraction."

With a smirk on his face, David says, "Distraction?" He rubs his forehead. "Mom hasn't left Dad's side since he's been in this hospital. When you're in a relationship..."

Before he can continue I interrupt him. "But that's it. We aren't in a relationship. She isn't ready for all that yet."

"But yet she drove over three hours to be here at the hospital." David adjusts in his seat again. I'm sure his height, a few inches taller than me, and his stature, much broader than mine is making it difficult for him to be comfortable in the seat. He finally stands and says, "I'm headed back to the room to relieve Chris. How about the two of you go to the house for a couple of hours then come back?"

Instead of rejecting I agree with a slight nod to my head. I look around the waiting room to check for anything we could have left behind. Other than food we haven't had much else in the room. I stack up a few bags of chips on a table, and if another family has to be here before we return, hopefully they'll help themselves.

"I hear we've been kicked out for a few hours." Chris says standing in the doorway of the waiting room.

"Yeah, but I'm not staying gone for too long. Leaving with him in this condition makes me nervous. Any change yet?" I walk toward Chris and we walk side-by-side out of the hospital.

"Nothing yet. The doctors came in to check on him, but didn't have much of an update. I can tell Mom is starting to get weary, almost as if she knows more than the doctors." He looks at me and says, "She doesn't seem optimistic."

I stop walking and look at Chris. "You're not helping." I point toward the hospital. "We should go back."

Chris grabs my shoulder and says, "Bryan at this point there isn't much more we can do from that waiting room." He pushes me forward toward the parking lot. "If he recovers, or not, we are going to need to help Mom. We'll have to step in as soon as she walks out of this hospital. She's going to be exhausted." Although I don't want to think about us leaving this hospital without my dad, I realize Chris is right.

During our drive back to the house Chris reminds me of our times growing up. His memories differing from mine because of our age difference. When I was running the street, and chasing behind chicks, Chris was at home in his younger years. Being the youngest, he was able to have our parents to himself.

"Dad must have grown tired over the years." I laugh. "You had it easy." Chris snickers. "Really, man. David probably had it the hardest. Just always had to be perfect in Dad's eyes. Then there was me who came along breaking all the rules."

"I appreciate his tough approach though." He looks from the road to me. "I think we turned out like decent dudes." Hitting my arm he says, "Even with you going on your passion adventure." Chris' eyes shift from me to the driveway when we pull up to our parent's house. I take a deep breath as I prepare myself to walk into the house. "Nice of Nicole to come here from Georgia to check on you."

I groan. "We only need to be here for a couple of hours." I warn Chris, "Don't get too comfortable."

The house is quiet and the lights are dim. Chris and I go our separate ways, both of us walking to our own rooms in the house. My room is empty and I'm relieved that I don't have to face Nicole again. Shrugging out of my shoes and pants and throwing my shirt in a pile on the floor, I climb into my bed and shut my eyes.

Chapter Twenty-Two
NICOLE

Laying uncomfortably on the couch I watch the ceiling and think how life could have been growing up in this house. I can't believe Bryan walked away from his family firm, the one that provided all of this. And now that I lay on this overstuffed couch I can't believe I hopped my ass in a car and drove to Tennessee.

The front door opens and I can hear people walk into the house but I don't move. After our breach of the security system, I decide to lay low until Laila and I return to the hospital. Instead of taking the bed Laila offered, I decided the couch would be the most appropriate. Laying in a random bed, in an unfamiliar house of a family I hardly know feels a lot like Goldilocks. And I pass.

As I hear the people take the staircase I wonder if Bryan is amongst the footsteps I hear. I selfishly want to see him, I want to wrap my arms around him and comfort him, but from our encounter earlier at the hospital I'll just give him his space. If he wanted me to comfort him I'd expect he'd come around; he hasn't been shy about that before.

My curiosity is getting the best of me and I would like to walk around the house and explore. Explore the world that Mr. Clark created and Mrs. Clark cared for all these years. Instead I shut my eyes tight and count the imaginary sheep bouncing around in my head. The living room lights flip on and I hear Laila's voice, "Hey, are you sleep?"

If she planned on whispering why the hell did she turn on the lights? "No, Laila. I'm wide awake. I can't sleep here." I turn on my side and watch her take a seat across from me in an overstuffed love seat. This room looks like it's hardly been visited, and is probably just a show room. I should have found the couch that everyone sits on, if one exists, to fall asleep. "It feels strange to be here for the first time under these circumstances."

"I've been here before and it still feels strange for me too." She looks toward the stairs. "Bryan and Chris came home but I don't think they plan on staying long. I came out of the room to let Chris rest." She takes a deep breath. "Before he laid down he said it's not looking good for his dad."

I gasp. "No, that's horrible. I couldn't imagine losing my dad at this age." I sit up on the couch and stare in the direction of the window where the intricately ordained curtains are closed shut.

"I just can't imagine how they are feeling right now. In the hospital I was thinking about my mom's hospital stay and all the emotions came flooding back." Laila stops and looks at me. "Bryan checked on me."

I smirk before I realize that wasn't necessary. "Sorry. But I probably shouldn't have come here unannounced." Laila shakes her head. "I don't think he was excited to see me."

Laila raises her eyebrows. "Think anyone would be excited in this time?"

"You have a point. I'm tripping." I grab a decorative

pillow from the couch and hold onto it. "This is going to be a difficult time." Laila nods her head. "How long are you staying?"

"I don't know. Maybe a couple of days. I talked to my manager and he said I can work from here for a few days." She picks at her shirt. "But working from here is difficult."

"I'm sure it is. Especially in the waiting room."

"What about you?" She crosses her legs in the chair.

Laughing I say, "I had no plan. I told my manager I'd be back in a couple of days." I scrunch my nose and say, "I wasn't even really sure how to explain my visit here."

"Like you're going to visit a friend's dad in the hospital. Simple, right?" Laila sounds much more at ease with this situation than I am. I've been overthinking every aspect of this visit. Had Bryan and I kept to my normal routine, casual fucking, I wouldn't be thinking this hard about being here. It would have been no big deal. But now that I've given up my bench of prospects and I'm trying to be a one-man woman, everything has come into question. In the past I could give two shits about how a guy was feeling about my actions. Whether he had feelings was not my concern.

Laila looks at me as I contemplate all these thoughts. "Looks like you need a drink, girl." She stands from her chair reaches for the pillow on my lap throwing it to the side. "Let's see what the Clarks have available." Her idea of easing my mind brings a wide grin to my face. I follow closely behind her to the kitchen. She stops walking and looks at me. "Personal space, damn Nicole."

With my hands in the air I say, "Something about this house makes me nervous."

"Something or someone?" she teases. I shrug my shoulders and she continues into the kitchen. "This seems like a house that would have a wine cellar or at least a bar." She looks around the kitchen through a few of the cabinets and says, "Where do you think it would be?"

"What are you looking for," I hear from behind me. I turn to face Bryan whose eyes are red and his clothes disheveled.

"Was trying to find an adult beverage." He points to the door and Laila follows his hand. "Ah," she says from the other room. "Jackpot." She returns with a decanter of brown liquor. "I think this will do." She opens the refrigerator and pulls out a couple of cans of soda.

Bryan sits on a barstool at the counter and watches as she pours a couple of glasses of the liquor. He doesn't speak another word but graciously takes the glass of liquor she offers him. After his first sip he says, "My dad would be disappointed that you added soda to this liquor."

Laila looks down at the decanter and says, "Not sure I can drink anything without chaser. My pallet isn't that sophisticated yet."

I take a sip from my glass, closing my eyes as I let the liquid seep down my throat. When I open my eyes, Bryan is staring at me. "Before we head back to the hospital, let me give you a tour of the house."

After another sip of my drink I nod my head and follow Bryan out of the kitchen. Walking through the many rooms I stay paces behind him as I admire the decor of the house. "Your mother has done an amazing job decorating."

Bryan doesn't respond. He continues walking and describing rooms. Then when we get to his father's office he takes a seat across from the desk. I walk around the room stopping in front of a wall full of accolades, some recognizing Mr. Clark individually but most recognizing his firm.

"Last time I was home, my dad asked about me leaving the company. Leaving Tennessee. And after explaining my goals for my art it seemed as if he understood." His head falls and his shoulders heave. When I hear him clear his throat I watch as the tears stream down his face.

I grab him by the shoulders and pull him into a hug. With his head resting against my stomach I rub the top of his head. It's during these times when words escape me. There isn't anything that I can verbalize to take his pain away. Unlike Laila, I haven't experienced my mom or dad being seriously sick. I definitely can't act like everything is going to be okay, because it's not and to say so would be foolish.

My shirt scoots up and Bryan's hands are on my back with his lips on my stomach. His tongue dips into my belly button. I lean closer into him with my hands down the back of his shirt and my lips kissing his neck. This is the language I'm fluent in; the actions may not remove the pain but can ease the stress. At least for now.

As I kneel down into his lap, he pushes my shirt over my head and with a thumb between my nipple and bra, he flicks the fabric aside. I moan as he takes my nipple into his mouth. His hands make their way to my waistband and I feel feather light touches while his teeth tug on my nipples.

He releases my nipple and looks up at me. "I'm sorry," he rolls his eyes. "I can't even believe I'm thinking about sexing you right now." He pulls my shirt down and stands me in front of him.

With my arms still draped over his shoulders I pull him into me again. "Don't worry about it." With a kiss to the top of his head I say, "Let's get out of here."

Bryan runs up the stairs and I find Laila in the kitchen. "How was the tour?" Laila wriggles her eyebrows. I sigh and put my head back. "Uh oh. Doesn't seem it was the tour you wanted." With my head draped down I shake my head. "I don't think any of us are going to get any sleep here."

"I think Bryan went up to grab Chris. We can head back

to the hospital." I don't plan to stay in Tennessee for long, and before I leave I should probably try to get some sleep. "I'll need to find some place to crash before I drive back to Georgia."

"Yeah driving back will be much different from me being a passenger on a flight." Laila walks out of the kitchen and I follow closely behind her. We stand at the bottom of the stairs and I take one last look at the immaculate house in case I'm never back for a visit.

Chris appears at the top of the stairs. "Y'all ready?" Watching him come down the stairs is like watching a sloth. I look at Laila sideways and she shrugs her shoulders. "We can ride together." When he reaches the bottom of the stairs he says, "Nicole, when you need your car we'll bring you back by the house." He looks between me and Laila. "If that's cool with you."

With Chris leading us to the car, Laila and I climb into the backseat. I assume Bryan will be joining us in the passenger seat. Bryan runs from the front door to the car. "David just called and said we need to hurry back." He climbs into the car and looks at Chris, "Do you need me to drive?" Chris starts the car and shakes his head. We peel off from the driveway and take off to the hospital. My heart begins to race as fast as the car is moving along the winding road. Laila grabs my hand and neither of us speak but I know both of us are praying that we make it in time for the guys to see their dad.

Before Chris can park I lean forward between the front seats. "Don't worry about parking. You two hop out and we'll park."

Between sniffles Laila grabs her purse with a tight grip. "Let's go before I lose my shit." None of the Clarks are in the waiting room when we arrive. I take a seat next to Laila and try to keep my leg from bouncing.

My stomach growls. "Think we can head to the cafeteria for something to eat?" Laila nods her head.

"It smells half decent." I grab a tray and look behind me and realize Laila has stopped walking. "You okay?" She looks across the cafeteria.

"That's Shelby." I follow her glance to the lady she was calling Shelby. "She came by to visit Bryan. His ex from college."

I look down at the clothes I am still wearing from my trip. "Wonder why she's here." Or like us she could know his dad may not make it. But who called her? An older woman walks beside her. Maybe her mom?

"Let's just get some food." Laila grabs a tray and we walk through the food line. When we sit down Shelby and the older woman walk over to our table on their way out of the cafeteria.

Because we haven't been introduced I continue eating as Shelby addresses Laila. "Hi. I believe you were here for Mr. Clark also?" Laila nods her head and looks across the table to me. "I'm Shelby, and this is my mother." She reaches her hand out to shake Laila's hand.

"Nice to meet you. This is Nicole." Shelby reaches out for my hand and we also shake.

"We'll be in the waiting room for a while. My mom was hoping to see Mrs. Clark."

"We just left from there and none of the family is in the waiting room, yet." Shelby looks at her mom.

"Okay dear." Shelby's mom pats her shoulder. "We'll just go home for now." I'm thankful her mom spares us from the awkwardness that would be all of us in the waiting room together. Shelby waves at us and they walk away.

"Could you imagine?" I say once they are no longer in earshot.

"Girl, no. It was awkward enough introducing her to

you." Laila looks down. "I wanted to tell her you were Bryan's girlfriend but..."

"The words got caught in your throat?" I laugh. "It would have been a lie anyway."

Laila rolls her eyes at me. We finish eating and head back to the waiting room where we find the brothers sitting. When Bryan looks at me, I inhale. Chris walks to Laila and before he can begin speaking I already know what he's going to say.

Chapter Twenty-Three
BRYAN

"Honey," my mom sits across from me. "You and your brother need to get back to your lives in New York." Chris and I have been in Tennessee since my dad got sick, stayed to help for the funeral arrangements, and both decided to stay to make sure my mom was okay. Chris has also been helping David get the records in order at the firm.

I look at my mom, who through it all manages to smile, and say, "Are you ready to get us out of here?"

"No, Bryan. It's been tough but we all need to get back to some sort of normalcy. Unless the two of you plan on moving back in, it's time to rip off the Band-Aid."

Despite being back in Tennessee I haven't taken a break from my art. I've actually painted more than I've done in a while, escaping to my apartment daily to create a new piece. "You know..."

My mom cuts me off before I can continue. "Boy, before your dad passed he had just become comfortable with the fact that you were going to be an artist." With her hand reaching out for mine she says, "Go be an artist."

"But I can be an artist anywhere. Maybe I should come

back for a while." Like everything else in my life, I hadn't thought out this plan. I'd need to get out of my lease in New York. Move all my stuff back to Tennessee and find a place to exhibit my art, but it all can be done.

"Here you go again, making spur of the moment decisions." My mom stands walking toward the windows of the kitchen. "I haven't shared this with anyone yet. But I'll be selling the house."

"What?" I jump up out of my seat and walk up behind my mom. "Is that what you want to do? We've lived here our entire lives, mom. Why would you want to sell?"

Without looking at me my mom says, "Even before your father passed we had talked about downsizing. He was going to start working less and we had plans to travel the world." The thought of my dad not getting to retire and live out his last days enjoying life with my mom tugs at my heart.

"And now?"

"I'm going to do it. I'm going to do everything your father promised me before he decided to go have that damn heart attack." My mom has hardly ever cursed, at least not around us. She turns to look at me. "And I suggest you continue doing what you had planned. If any of us should have learned anything from your father's death, it's that life is short and we need to enjoy it. Tomorrow is not promised and although we shouldn't just make rash decisions, we shouldn't wait our whole lives to do what we would enjoy."

I understand exactly what my mom is trying to tell me. "You're right mom." I nod my head. "You're right."

"And while I'm on my soap box, between my travels it would be nice to come home to some grand-babies." She looks at me with a wide grin. "That girl who drove all the way from Georgia." She holds up two fingers. "Twice. Do right by her."

Smiling I say, "Nicole. I don't even know if she wants to be with me. And I've done a horrible job of showing her I want her lately."

My mom pats my shoulder. "No time like the present my dear. Tell her you want to be with her. You may not have finished college but you know how to use your words." I smirk at her low blow about college. "Then show her. Show her that you care about her."

"Okay mom. Seems like you are handling this situation much better than I am, obviously."

"Don't get me wrong, Bryan, it's hard. Each day will be a new challenge. Each milestone without your father will be tough. But if I live life as if I died that day, what would be the point of living?"

She walks away from me but before leaving the kitchen she looks back at me and says, "So you and Chris need to have your stuff all packed up and ready to go soon. The house will be on the market next week." She leaves the kitchen and I feel better about leaving my mom, but now I don't know what's next.

I walk to my room to do as my mom says and pack my shit up. I find my phone to call Nicole. She should be at work but I don't want to wait till she's off to let her know how I feel. Like my mom said, there's no time like the present.

"Hello."

"Hey, are you busy?"

"Not too much, just heading out of a meeting about to leave for the day." My bravery has subsided and she says, "Are you okay?"

"Yes. No. I mean I've been out of touch with you for weeks."

"Bryan."

"Wait, I know it's been a lot going on. And first, let me

thank you. You didn't have to come to Tennessee, let alone twice. Thank you."

"You don't have to thank me. That's what, that's what friends do."

"Friends?" I was hoping we could be more than that. "That's what I wanted to talk to you about."

"Okay."

"Would you be willing to..." When I consider asking her to be my girl over the phone after weeks of not talking to her I feel lame. "Could we try for more than friends?"

"I'm still in Georgia." She sighs. "And you're. You're not."

Before I commit to moving to Georgia without thinking about it I close my mouth. My mom is right, I make rash decisions before thinking them through. Instead, I ask if we can at least try.

"I'm willing to try." She laughs. "Besides my bench is empty and was starting to get a little cold." I laugh knowing how difficult that's probably been with me avoiding her for weeks. "Call me later?"

"Sure will." I finish grabbing my clothes that have been scattered around my room since I've been home. I've moved most of my childhood things out of my room over the years since leaving the house, but I do another check of my room. I can't believe when I leave this time it could be the last. But I understand my mom needing to leave. I haven't been able to enter my dad's office since the funeral. I'm sure, for my mom, it's the same experience with most of the house.

"Yo, you packing up?" Chris plops onto my bed. "When are you leaving?"

"I haven't decided yet. But Mom gave me the 'you ain't gotta go home, but you gotta get the hell outta here' speech today."

Chris squints. "She did?" I nod my head. I'm hesitant to

fill him in on the rest of our discussion. "Guess I better get my shit together before she has to give me the same speech." Chris laughs. "I thought we'd need to stick around longer to make sure Ma was okay."

"I was thinking the same thing." I sit across from Chris at my desk. "She's definitely doing better than I am with all of this."

"Maybe we can catch the same flight back?" I haven't decided where I'm going yet. After my mom schooled me about my outlook on a relationship I may reconsider New York. But for now, I need to get back and plan an exhibit before I'm broke.

"I think I'll book a flight for Saturday." Chris claps his hands and I say, "Want me to book yours too?"

"Yeah, I'm missing my girl like crazy. And now that I know Ma is ready for us to get gone I can get home and try to get back to my routine."

When Chris leaves my room, I book our flights back to New York, grab my keys and head to my condo. I need pictures of the art I've created over the weeks. I'll leave the pieces here till I have more details about this exhibit I'll pull together. Looking at the piece still on my easel, I remember the artist Nicole and I met in Atlanta. Her exhibit was breathtaking, and inspiring. If I could produce the same ambience my exhibit will be a success.

I've never planned an exhibit because most of my art has been sold to individual buyers through word of mouth. I open my notepad app on my phone and take down a few things I need to look into, people I need to contact. Then I call Nicole.

"Look at you calling like you said you would."

"Of course I'm calling. You'll get tired of hearing my voice soon enough." I laugh into the speakerphone. "I'm headed back to New York this weekend."

"For real?" Nicole's voice raises an octave. "Already?" I

tell her about my conversation with my mom, minus the piece about her. "Sounds like your mom is doing better than expected. That's good to hear." While Nicole was in Tennessee she didn't spend a ton of time with my mom, but the time they did interact was enough to leave an impression on both of them.

"Now that I'm going back to reality I need to sell some work before I'm a starving artist for real." Nicole laughs. "Unless you're willing to share your apartment with me."

"I did say my bench was getting cold." Nicole laughs. "Let me know if there is anything I can do to help you though." Nicole's willingness to help me with my dream amazes me, especially after seeing Shelby and being reminded how much she doesn't believe in me as an artist.

"Actually, do you have the info for the artist we saw at the exhibit? The one where you bought the art?"

"Yes. I do. I'll text you the details." She catches me up on the past weeks, and before we hang up I promise I'll call her daily. I'd rather see her then talk to her on the phone. Like her I'm not sure if I can maintain a long-distance relationship. I already feel like I'm going through pussy withdrawals.

On our flight back to New York I rattle off a list of things I could use Chris' help with coordinating. My mom gave me a good idea for the exhibit and now I just need to execute. "Are you ready for all of this?" Chris asks.

Looking at him like he's talking out of the side of his neck I reply, "Are you ready for all of this?" Grabbing our bags from baggage claim we are surprised to see Laila holding a sign that reads 'Clark Brothers.' I know Chris is excited to see his girl, but I'm strangely excited to see her too. Maybe because I know we are getting back to our routine. With me as the third wheel on this cart of love, I happily follow behind the two of them.

Laila turns to me and says, "My bad, Bryan. I almost

forgot to give you a hug. I was too excited to see your brother." She wraps me in her arms and I know she genuinely loves my brother and by default has love for me too.

"I won't blame you this time." I tap the top of her head. "As long as you can pull off your part for this exhibit I won't hold it against you."

She points to herself. "Consider it done. My job is easy." She looks between me and Chris. "Y'all two have much more to get done."

"And we have to make sure it's all a success. I just spent too many weeks with you to have you back on our couch," Chris says with more enthusiasm than necessary. Success or fail, this exhibit will be the start of something amazing.

Chapter Twenty-Four
NICOLE

Bryan has kept his promise, or slight threat, to call me daily. Some days he calls multiple times a day. After weeks of not talking to him, hearing his voice excites me but not seeing him is making our phone conversations difficult. I can only sext and listen to him seduce me over the phone for so long. I've changed the batteries in my side table toy enough times for batteries to be a staple on my grocery list.

When Bryan told me he decided to have his art exhibit in Atlanta I had to change my panties. I'm excited to see his art, but even more excited to get him in my bed.

The knock at my door startles me and I run to peep through the hole before pulling the door open. "Laila?" I open the door and she wraps me in her arms.

"Thought if I surprised you I could catch you before you made plans to ditch me for payback." She laughs and throws her duffle bag on the floor.

"You and your people are infamous for these surprise visits. What are you doing here?"

"I didn't want to miss Bryan's first art exhibit." Her

smile is suspect. "We have a room downtown near the exhibit but I wanted to see you before then." I haven't seen or heard from Bryan today but I assumed I wouldn't see him until tonight although he's been in town all week. He declined my offer to help get things set up and it's probably for the better. I doubt I would have been able to let him focus, at least not until I've had my fix.

"Chris is with Bryan?" I lead Laila to my couch and I take a seat. Laila stands staring at the art on my wall, the art Bryan created and hung last time he was here.

"He's very talented. He shouldn't have a hard time selling all of his pieces tonight." I hope he is successful tonight, although his alternative of crashing with me wouldn't be too bad either.

"I can't wait to see the rest of the pieces. Before him I wasn't as interested in art as I am now." Laila sits beside me and looks at me with her goofy grin again. "Okay, what's up? You are horrible at keeping secrets."

"No secrets here. Just happy you finally decided to give Bryan a chance. All these random dudes." She rolls her eyes. "Wasting your time."

"Yeah we'll see. Little kitty isn't enjoying this long-distance situation. It's one thing to not have anyone around worth sexing but to have someone I can't get to on the regular." I smirk at her. "You remember how that was."

"You'll be good." Laila stands up and walks toward my bedroom. "Give me a tour." My apartment is larger than Laila's quaint New York space but not by much. In my room she stops in front of the outfit I have laid out on my bed. "Is this what you are wearing tonight?" I nod my head. I decided to wear a geometric print, mid-knee dress with a pair of calf length boots and a pair of tights that match the print of the dress. "Artsy."

"Felt appropriate. What are you wearing tonight?" She describes her skinny jeans and off shoulder sweater with heels that I'm sure she'll rock like she's straight out of New York. Since graduating, her style has evolved and I'm happy because that plain Jane motif she had at L. U. was wack. "I think we should have a celebratory glass of wine."

In the kitchen I open a bottle of Moscato and pour us both a glass. "The only thing missing is Jennifer and Monica."

I run to the couch and grab my phone. "They can be here in spirit." I video call Jennifer and tell her to get Monica on her phone. With all of us in the room we make plans for a reunion trip in the new year. We also promise to call them tonight when we get to the exhibit.

After a last look in the mirror, I pat my stomach. For some reason my nerves are getting the best of me. My outfit looks amazing, my hair is perfectly coiled, and my make-up is flawless, but I feel like something is missing. Laila looks over my shoulder and says, "Butterflies?"

"Don't think I've ever felt this nervous about seeing a guy."

Laila pulls one of my coils and says, "That's understandable. It's been years since you've been in an actual relationship." I scrunch my nose. "Or whatever the two of you want to call what y'all are doing." Laila's phone rings and she claps her hands. "Our ride is here." I sigh and grab my purse.

"Our ride?"

"Just go with it." I follow Laila out of the apartment and after locking up, follow her down the stairs to a waiting black town car. The driver opens the door and Laila instructs me to scoot into the car.

"All this for an art exhibit?" Laila shrugs. "I could get used to this treatment though."

The parking lot of the art gallery is packed. "Wow. There are a lot of people here." The driver opens the door and my nerves are on overdrive.

Unlike the last time I was here in the gallery, the ambience is much more romantic. Last time the mood was more realistic with images of everyday life. The lighting was bright and street music was playing. Now the lights are dim, and I can hear R&B playing softly. Chris greets us at the door and leads us into the main section of the exhibit. Looking around the gallery I realize the art looks familiar, at least the main subject of the art. With my eyes squinted I ask Chris, "Are these all of..."

"Of you?" Bryan wraps his arm around my shoulder. "My favorite muse." I look at him with my mouth agape. "Do you like them?"

"They are gorgeous." Bryan wraps me in his arms and leads me around the remainder of the gallery. I recognize the background of many of the pieces. "When did you have the time to do all of these?"

He looks down and says, "When I wasn't talking to you, you were the only thing on my mind." I throw my arms around his neck and pull him into a kiss.

"Hey, we don't need live action art." I release Bryan and see David standing behind him. "Everyone is already raving about the pieces." He points toward Chris who looks like he's managing a few people. "You've already sold half of the pieces."

Bryan smiles and kisses my forehead. "I won't have to crash your place after all." My frown gives away my disappointment before I realize I'm pouting. "You don't look happy about that."

"Guess having you nearby wouldn't have been the worst thing that could have happened."

"Let me show you my favorite piece." Bryan grabs my hand and leads me to a crowded space. He excuses us through the people standing around. When we get to the front his mother turns and smiles.

She reaches out to me and I walk into her arms. "Mrs. Clark, how are you?"

"Tonight I'm doing great. Bryan did an amazing job with all these pieces." She points to the wall, "This one is my absolute favorite." On the wall hangs a painting of me leaning over his mother with my hand on her shoulder. We were in the hospital the day his father passed away. I didn't realize Bryan was around during that moment.

"I agree." We stand admiring the painting until we hear noise behind us causing both of us to turn around. He's there on one knee with a box outstretched and all the people crowded around start clapping. My hand shoots to my mouth and my eyes grow wide.

"In this moment, as we celebrate Our Reason, I want you to know that you are my reason." Chris takes Laila's hand in his and continues to describe his love for her while tears stream down her cheeks. From the corner of my eye I spot Laila's family watching intently. "Will you marry me?"

Laila starts jumping up and down and screams, "Of course."

As they hug, Mrs. Clark leans into my ear and whispers, "That boy always knows how to steal someone's thunder."

Laughing I look around to find Bryan and the smile spread across his face proves he doesn't mind sharing the spotlight. I walk over to Laila's family and give each of them hugs. Mrs. Jackson kisses my cheek and says, "Maybe the two of you will be in-laws." I pull away from her and smile. She and Laila think alike and their optimism is cute.

I run up to Laila and wrap her in my arms. Pulling away I grab her hand and admire her new bling. "Congrats, heffa!" I dig my phone from my pocket. "The girls are going to kill me. I should have recorded."

Laila looks around the room. "I'm hoping someone caught it on their phone."

Chris joins us and says, "What's wrong?"

"We forgot to record for the girls to see." I say as I unlock my phone to call them.

Chris smiles and turns around. "In person was probably better anyway." Laila screams as Jennifer and Monica walk out from the crowd. We hug and chastise them for keeping us in the dark about their visit.

Monica cuts her eyes at me and says, "And ruin all this sweetness." With her hand in the air she wags her finger. "But we are only here for the night, so although I'm sure the two of you had plans of returning the romance, we need to get out and celebrate." Jennifer agrees.

"Maybe just a drink or two." Laila says looking at Chris with a wide grin.

"Have fun, babe. We have forever together." Jennifer and Monica act as if they are gagging and roll their eyes. Chris laughs. "Too much?" Monica puts her fingers up, mimicking a pinch.

"Let me just fill in Bryan on the plans." Not like Bryan has to rush off to a job, but I'm not sure how long I have him here in Atlanta.

Bryan is describing a piece to a younger lady. With her eyes full of amazement she follows his hand as he points out different aspects of the art, the most amazing part being he does this all from memory. Once he's done describing the piece, one I remember distinctively, me in my blue dress when I was visiting Laila in New York, I tell him I'll be joining the ladies for a couple of drinks and ask him his plans for the night.

"If it's fine with you, I'll be at your apartment waiting on you." I wink at him and he says, "I have to wrap up here but I should be there when you get back." I peck his lips before I turn to walk away.

Chapter Twenty-Five
BRYAN

Nicole answers the door wearing a silk robe. Unlike earlier her face is bare and her hair is wilder. She stares at me before inviting me into her apartment. I thought I had the willpower to wait until after I gave her my news to devour her but my body has a mind of its own. My lips crash onto hers in the doorway. I don't even wait until the door is closed behind us. These past few weeks of teasing each other over the phone were tense. I thought I'd have to visit the doctor for a cure to my blue balls.

Her hands grab my head and we kiss intently while I untie her robe and let it fall to the ground. The door slams behind us and before moving I make sure it's locked. Picking her up, I balance her against the door and kiss down her body. I didn't expect her to be naked under the robe but I'm glad I don't have to fumble with her underwear. My fingers rub across her clit and she's already moist. A sound escapes my throat that I don't even recognize. I wrap her legs around me and walk her to the bedroom where I place her onto the bed. I undress, grabbing a condom from my pocket before matching her nakedness.

When I look at the seductive smile on her face, it makes my dick jump. She giggles and I climb on top of her. "Damn, Nicole." She kisses me, her tongue as deep in my throat as my mouth will allow. I slide into her and our rhythm is frantic, neither of us finding a cadence. I try to slow down to allow us to enjoy the ride. After our wait, I don't want to rush the pleasure. Then she thrusts her hips into me and I lose my resolve. She clenches her muscles around my dick and I lose it. With my body quivering I collapse on top of her. She kisses me down my neck and I move beside her. With my arm wrapped around her bare belly I say, "We'll need another round."

Nicole lays her head on my chest. "I agree. We need a round to celebrate all the great things that happened tonight." There is definitely plenty to celebrate. The art exhibit was a success, with most of my pieces going at prime asking price but more so, Nicole being surprised by the pieces I chose to display; the smile on my mom's face, her brief reprieve from her mourning; then the grand finale, Chris proposing to Laila, finally. "You outdid yourself with the exhibit."

Laughing I ask, "Because you were featured in all the pieces?"

She slaps my chest. "It helps, but the pieces were nothing short of amazing. And I'm so happy everyone who was there was able to witness your creativity."

"Thank you. I really appreciate your support."

"How long do I get to appreciate you here in Atlanta?" She sits up on her elbows and stares into my eyes.

"For as long as you can stand." Her head turns to the side. "I decided I can do art anywhere. And what better place than the place of my muse." Nicole's mouth drops and I cover it with mine. It's time for another round of our celebrations.

The End

☆☆☆☆☆

As an Indie author, I appreciate you taking a leap of faith to read my work. I'm truly honored that you not only purchased the book, but you also finished the book. Now that you've read the book, and I hope love it, I need you to leave a review and tell a friend.

You purchasing the book is like a warm day in the middle of winter.

You finishing the book is like a chocolate chip cookie fresh out of the oven.

You leaving a review and telling a friend is like a child saying I love you...unsolicited. Just warms my heart.

And I live for warm heart moments, so tell me what you think. Good, bad, or indifferent I want to hear from you.

You can leave a review on Amazon or Goodreads and let me, and other book lovers, know how much you loved the book. If you are looking for your next book to read you can also visit my blog at www.NotTheLastPage.com for book reviews.

Want to know, before everyone else, when I'm releasing a new book? Join my mailing list at www.NotTheLastPage.com/ByJ_Nichole.

We can also connect on my Facebook page at www.facebook.com/byjnichole, or Twitter @by_jnichole

ALSO BY J. NICHOLE

Freshmen Fifteen

Sophisticated Sophomore

Summer Fling

Grown & Sexy Senior

Christmas Secrets: A Black Family Christmas

ABOUT THE AUTHOR

J. Nichole received her bachelor's degree in Computer Information Systems from Florida A&M University and a master's degree in Management Information Systems from the University of Illinois at Springfield.

J. Nichole has spent the past ten years as an IT Consultant. She is married with one daughter.

For more information:
www.NotTheLastPage.com

Made in the USA
Columbia, SC
14 March 2018